THE MYSTERY OF THE
Stolen Statue

BOOKS IN THE CASEY AND THE CLASSIFIEDS SERIES

B O O K   O N E

T H E   M Y S T E R Y   O F   T H E
Stolen Statue

T R A C Y   G R O O T

CROSSWAY BOOKS • WHEATON, ILLINOIS
A DIVISION OF GOOD NEWS PUBLISHERS

The Mystery of the Stolen Statue

Copyright © 1996 by Tracy Groot

Published by Crossway Books
       a division of Good News Publishers
       1300 Crescent Street
       Wheaton, Illinois 60187

Cover illustration: Bruce Emmett

Cover design: Cindy Kiple

First printing, 1996

Printed in the United States of America

Library of Congress Cataloging-in-Publication Data
Groot, Tracy, 1964-
   The mystery of the stolen statue / Tracy Groot.
      p.   cm.—(Casey and the Classifieds ; bk. 1)
   Summary: Casey and her friends form an organization called the
Classifieds and set out to find and retrieve a wood carving stolen
from a teacher.
   ISBN 0-89107-874-6
   [1. Mystery and detective stories.]   I. Title II. Series.
PZ7.G8955Myf 1996
[Fic]—dc20   96-24065

04		03		02		01		00		99		98		97		96
15	14	13	12	11	10	9	8	7	6	5	4	3	2	1

For my mom and dad

*The author would like to thank Jacob Groot
for his memories of wartime Holland
and of a certain boy named Kees.
May this book be your family's tree.*

Chapter One

■

I SAT ON THE COUCH AND PRETENDED TO LOOK EXTREMELY absorbed in my mythology book for Mr. Black's class. It had to look good so my mom wouldn't ask me to do any folding. Occasionally I would mutter something like, "Icarus, Icarus . . . Oh yeah, the feathers and wax guy." Childish, but it got me out of the folding.

Actually, I was waiting. Just like my older brother Tony. He sat cross-legged on the floor with a ton of homework. He'd ruffle through some papers, chew on his pencil, consult a few notes. He didn't fool me in the least. He knew what time it was.

Then it came. The *thump* on the front porch.

Slowly I looked up from my place on the couch to lock eyes with Tony. We stared at each other, squinty-eyed, and planned our moves. A dog barked. A distant siren wailed. Mom called from downstairs for the bleach. Neither of us twitched.

Tension crackled in the room; adrenaline surged in our veins. The staredown lasted a few . . . more . . . critical . . . seconds—and the race was on! I leapt from the couch with a whoop and sailed over the ottoman. Tony scrambled up from the floor.

"Forget it, little sister! It's all mine!" Tony roared.

"Not this time!"

I was two steps ahead of him, shrieking all the way to the front door because Tony is the size of a Forty-niner halfback and although it's great to win these races, I do have an aversion to pain. I'm willing to accept defeat if it means I'll spare myself some agony.

But I am willing to sacrifice my No Pain Policy if I haven't won a race in a while. My pride is worth occasional pain.

So when Tony swiped me aside into the wall I took it like a trooper and shoved right back into him. That caught him off guard—he's aware of my No Pain Policy—and he stumbled. I shot past him, pushed past the screen door, and snatched up the *Hamilton Daily*. Victory was mine!

I did a little dance, made some crowd-goes-wild noises, and generally made a fool of myself in front of Mr. Sanchez, our next-door neighbor. He's used to us though and gave me no more than a glance from his bushes. He keeps his bushes so manicured, they could hurt someone.

Tony leaned against the door, panting and grinning. "Don't let it go to your head. Sports section please."

I followed him back into the house, where Mom's request for the bleach took on a dangerous tone. Tony ran off to get it from the garage. I tossed the sports section on the floor and settled down on the couch with my own section. The classifieds.

I start with the obituaries first. It's interesting to see the ages of the recently deceased. "Bloom, Phillip. 25. Passed away unexpectedly Wednesday evening."

The "passed away unexpectedlies" intrigue me the most. Car accident? Drowning? Or perhaps something more sinister. Maybe he was the briefcase type, on his way to the office when he noticed a dark car following him . . .

I don't dwell on the obits very long because sometimes they're depressing. "Carlisle, Lisa Marie. 2 months. Beloved only child of Daniel and Angela Carlisle." *Gulp*. Moving right along.

Then come the personal ads, my favorites.

Tony came back from his errand and sat on the floor, paging through the sports section. I skimmed the personals because most were carryovers from yesterday's paper. I did read one to Tony, though, because it bewildered me.

"Tone, listen to this. 'To the man in the orange VW: the rain in Spain stays mainly on the plain.' What on earth is that supposed to mean?" I leaned back on the couch and stared up at the ceiling. Big mistake. I make a move like that and I'm pegged.

Tony may be big and appear not-too-bright, but looks are deceiving. "I don't know," he replied, totally serious. "Sounds cryptic to me. If you analyze it, it could contain an exposé of our entire U.S. defense system."

He knows how to push my buttons. And I bought it—hook, line, and stinking sinker.

"No kidding? It's probably in code!" I started to get excited, my brain whirring a mile a minute. Then I caught Tony's expression and could have—well, I was mad!

It all started when I was about eight years old. I like to think about things—examine possibilities. So sue me. My older brother caught on to this and from then on lived his life to humiliate me to dust when he caught me dreaming. I don't know what the big deal is. If something fascinates me enough to make me want to ponder it, why should he feel driven to ridicule me for it? Dad calls it insecurity, which amazes me. Tony insecure? Ha.

The guy is not only good-looking (so people tell me), but he's smart, funny, and can do perfect impressions of every single faculty or staff member at Beverly High, right down to the guy who delivers the milk cartons every week. Dad says my Dream States (Dream State: the time during which a subject is pondered—i.e., dreamed about. Even Tony wouldn't mention that term to his friends. It's kind of a family thing) make Tony feel like he's missing something. He says Tony may think fast, but he doesn't dream.

Tony's highest joy is to bait me, but on rare occasions I've actually had decent conversations with him. I've lured him into discussions on, for example, the possibility of separate universes existing in a speck of dust. He'd cock an eyebrow, offer a comment or two. But just when he'd start to get interesting, he'd catch himself and bail out of the conversation.

So when I looked over at him from the couch, I was fit to be tied. I make an honest effort to control my temper, but consider the circumstance. I've heard something about the patience of Job, but I'll bet even Job wanted to belt someone once in a while.

This time I settled for heaving a couch pillow at my brother. Not very satisfying. It only poofed off him like a—well, like a couch pillow off a halfback.

I snapped my paper like I've seen my dad do and haughtily turned my attention back to the classifieds. I skimmed the lost and founds, most of them carryovers too, until the last ad caught my eye.

LOST: SMALL, OLD WOODEN CARVING OF A SHEP-HERD BOY. SENTIMENTAL VALUE ONLY. $500.00 REWARD. LAST SEEN IN BEVERLY HIGH SCHOOL. CONTACT JOHN TEN BRINK, 555-6472.

I kept a very careful poker face. I have no idea what a

poker face is except that's what my dad calls it when he knows I'm trying hard not to reveal another Dream State.

The questions formed faster than I could speculate answers for them. A silly wooden carving worth five hundred bucks to someone? How could a person lose a decoration like that? People lose rings, car keys, wallets—not carvings. Sentimental value only? Yeah, right.

Maybe it had a secret opening in it, with a safe-deposit box key shoved inside. Maybe it was carved from some infinitely valuable wood . . . from the *Mayflower* maybe. Or maybe some pilgrim carved it *on* the *Mayflower*.

If it really *was* sentimental value, why a carving of a shepherd boy? What did it mean to the owner? Was it his son? Did his only son carve it for him, then die in some tragic accident? I shook my head. I liked the safe-deposit box idea better. The *contents* of the safe-deposit box—that was what interested me. I was just about to explore this curious avenue when it hit me like a pop quiz. Ten Brink. Beverly High School. It could be none other than—

"Tony, who did you have for history last year?"

"Ten Brink."

"Holy cow," I wheezed.

Tony gave me a look. "It's nothing to get excited about. I hear he's supposed to retire. He could have done me a favor and retired last year."

"Listen to this . . ."

I read him the ad. And what do you know—Anthony Edward DeWinter actually laid down the sports section, sat back, and reflected. No smart-aleck smirk. No demoralizing quip. In a delicate, sacred moment I saw in Tony's eyes a spark. I pretended not to notice.

"Five hundred bucks for a piece of wood," Tony murmured. "What could it possibly mean to him?"

"Maybe the wood is really valuable?" I offered cautiously. I had to be careful here. Let Tony do the talking. Protect this thing like a candle in a hurricane.

"No, not the wood itself," Tony began in a big-brother, know-it-all tone I normally hate but found forgivable given the circumstance. "The person who made the carving . . . or who gave it to him. That's why it's 'sentimental value only.' Trouble is, it's pretty hard to imagine Mr. Ten Brink being sentimental over *anything*."

"What's he like?"

Tony made a disrespectful noise and said, "You haven't seen him before?"

"Of course I've *seen* him."

"Well he's *like* exactly what he *looks* like."

I considered this. Hmm . . . Mr. John Ten Brink, teacher of eleventh-grade history and twelfth-grade American government. I pictured him walking down the hallway, and with this mental image I could understand Tony's statement.

Suspicion seemed to be Mr. Ten Brink's most noticeable characteristic. Not the nervous kind, but cold suspicion. As if he knew every person he saw had something to hide, something they should be ashamed of. Sounds crazy, but this is the impression I had. I think almost everybody is afraid of him. Kids don't say "hi" to him in the hallway—they only nod. Because they know that's all he'll do in return.

He's tall, almost as tall as my dad, but stooped a little in an old-age way. His eyes are sky-blue and kind of watery, like my grandmother's. His hair is very thick and white. He wears large, square-shaped glasses a generation or two out of style. And he wears a constant frown. Scowl is a better word.

His accent, Dutch or German, gets thicker when he's angry. Kids are sure he mutters swear words in some foreign language after yelling at them for a poorly done assignment.

Despite his formidable appearance, I've always felt rather sorry for him. I don't know why. Maybe because he knows kids mock him and don't like him. Maybe it's just my underdog mentality. I always root for the losers. Another policy of mine. Except if the losers are playing against the Beverly High football team; then I root for Tony. I know my priorities.

"Sentimental value only," I heard Tony mutter as he stared at the ceiling fan.

A knock at the door ruined what opportunity I had to make the most of the situation. I wanted to discuss at length a plan of action to hunt for the shepherd boy and split the reward, as well as further possibilities on the carving's curious worth. Tony got up to answer the door, and I could tell by his face as he passed me that he'd already forgotten the carving.

Mike Pulaski stood at the door, football in hand. Needing no further invitation, Tony went outside to toss some passes with his friend.

I sighed. I'd have to take up this issue with my best friend, Marty Behrens. He's been my best friend since third grade. I know, I know—sooner or later we're going to have to deal with the fact that he's a guy and I'm a girl. Thankfully, neither one of us has raised this issue yet. We don't want to. We would have to face the fact that there isn't much room in a grown-up world for best friends who are opposite genders. (I say "gender" because I hate saying the *s* word. It's on my list of hated words. Like *nostril* and *pus*.)

At the end of the last school term I discovered a transfer student from Hiawatha who could be considered my second best friend. Jackie D'Amico. I met her in home ec, the one and only class I ever flunked. She's the bravest person I've ever met. She put an end to Katie Wentworth's torment of Esther Zimmerman.

Katie's most common method of harassment (and least imaginative if you ask me) was to chew up wads of paper, then toss the gummy spitballs into Esther's hair. Esther, a pathetic heap of misery, would only look down and lift a hand now and then to brush off the wads. Although I felt sorry for her, I was angry at her as well. At least I stand up for myself, even if I'm scared senseless. Esther never does.

If Mrs. Simmons, our home ec teacher, ever knew the daily dramas going on in the back of her classroom, she never let on. The torment continued while she blathered away about tomato delight and no-fail pie crust.

Then came The Incident. One day while Mrs. Simmons and another student pulled a huge mess of taffy, Katie Wentworth amused herself by dropping pinches of eraser filings down the back collar of Esther's shirt. I heard a chair slide back, looked over my shoulder, and knew something wonderful was about to happen.

The new girl rose from her last-row seat and walked three desks down until she stood behind Katie's desk. The front half of the class watched the taffy. The back half of the class watched in awe as the transfer student from Hiawatha stood motionless with arms folded behind the toughest, meanest girl in eighth grade.

I had a great view, one seat back and kitty-corner to Katie. I stared in wonder at the new kid's face. Her pretty brown eyes shone with vengeance—a grim, awesome, fearless vengeance.

I could tell something didn't seem right to Katie. She paused with a pinch of filings en route to Esther's collar and ever so slowly turned her head. She saw the folded arms first. Her eyes traveled up to see who owned the arms. One look at the smoldering face, and Katie Wentworth knew Judgment Day had visited Beverly High.

I swallowed a Sweet-Tart whole. My underdog mentality rose in token protest against Katie's obvious doom, but I squashed it like an ant. I was going to enjoy this.

A fist fight? Pushing, shoving, swearing? We waited with shrieking nerves.

The new girl leaned forward until her nose was an inch from Katie's. "Don't you ever, *ever* bother her again," she hissed in a menacing rasp.

No threat. No promise of bodily harm. A simple command and Katie obeyed. The filings drained from her fingers while she stared, mesmerized, at the fury-filled eyes. The girl punctuated her point by standing there a full minute, even after Katie looked away.

Katie hasn't bothered Esther since. I introduced myself to Jackie that afternoon with enthusiasm bordering on hero worship. I've learned since then that she despises violence, has never hit a person in her life (she has no siblings), and resorts only to intimidation tactics when the occasion calls for it. She could have won an Oscar for that scene.

I got up from the couch and fished a pair of scissors out of the kitchen junk drawer. I clipped out the classified ad and reread it before I tucked it in my mythology textbook.

"Five hundred bucks for a piece of wood," I muttered. That could keep a person in Milky Ways for a long, long time.

Chapter Two

■

SO I GET DONE BAGGING HER GROCERIES, RIGHT?" MARTY SAID TO me as I whizzed through the combination on my locker. "Next thing I know, I'm standing there like an idiot while this old lady straightens the part in my hair with *her* comb."

I had no time to spare for sympathy. I took the ad out of my notebook and handed it to him. I snatched my French book and spiral binder. I replaced the ad when he finished reading it, and we took off at a fast trot down the hallway.

Marty whistled. "Mr. Ten Brink? Wow. Five hundred smackers."

"I'm gonna talk to him after class."

"You're *what*?"

"About the carving."

"You're not serious."

"Absolutely. Aren't you curious? Where it came from, who carved it. You know."

"Not enough to face that guy," he snorted. "I just hope you make it out of there alive."

"Oh please. He's probably got a lot of kids looking for it."

"It's different with you. You're *curious*. Big difference. He doesn't seem the type to invite a conversation about something personal."

I shrugged. "Why not? He placed the ad. What's so personal about that? Besides, who says I'm not going to look for it?"

Marty sighed. "I knew you'd say that. Why do I have the feeling I'm going to regret this?"

"Because you're going to help me. Tony already refused. We'll split the reward. Or maybe divide it three ways, 'cause I'm going to tell Jackie."

Though I had tried to pick up where Tony and I had left off, my bratty brother had no further interest in the carving. He probably cleared his head when he threw passes with Mike. Just as well, I had informed him with a toss of my head, I'd squander the reward all myself.

Marty and I reached a hallway intersection, and I waved as I continued one way while he turned the other.

Since a sub in French class showed us a film we'd already seen, I used the time productively and compiled a list of questions for Mr. Ten Brink. I figured if I went in there acting like an investigator, he wouldn't mind if I slipped in a question or two of personal interest.

Wrong, wrong, wrong.

His manner should have tipped me off when I slipped into his classroom after school let out. He sat at his desk and stared at a paper in his hand, his thick eyebrows set in a ferocious V. I didn't know if I should interrupt him or not, so I simply stood and waited. Mistake number one.

After three or four awkward minutes, he finally turned to me and said grumpily, "Well? What is it? Are you making a career of standing, or do you need something?"

"I—I . . . that is, I was j—j—just—" I stammer when I'm flustered.

"Red ink."

"Excuse me?"

Mr. Ten Brink flung the paper onto the desk. "Red ink. They do it to annoy me. Don't ever turn in a paper written in red ink."

"No, sir."

"Are you here about the carving?"

"Yes," I whispered weakly.

"It's been found." He turned back to his papers.

Found. That's it. The neat list of questions I clutched—all the mystery, all the intrigue—it was all for nothing. Disappointment must have curdled my brains because I should have run screaming from the room and never looked back. Instead, I didn't move.

Mr. Ten Brink noticed. This time when he turned to me, the ferocious V lifted into a straight line.

"Found," he repeated.

My tongue betrayed me by anchoring itself to the roof of my mouth and denying me the chance to say, "Why, that's just splendid, Mr. Ten Brink. I'm delighted you found your shepherd boy. Have a nice day."

Mr. Ten Brink appeared to be a little concerned.

"Is there anything else, young lady?"

Now or never. Do or die. Walk out now and you'll never know.

"Did your only son carve the shepherd?" The question shot out of me like a renegade popcorn kernel.

The eyebrows flew up. Now *he* was tongue-tied.

"What I mean is," I continued hastily, "who made the carving? My brother Tony says that's the real question, not the carving itself. Because for five hundred bucks, *he* could carve you one."

Mr. Ten Brink studied me, and so help me I studied him

back. It was an awesome, scary moment as I held my ground and waited for answers.

"Your Tony is a wise boy."

"Yes, he is," I encouraged.

"Tony DeWinter."

"Yes!" I enthused. We were on a roll.

"Good kid. You look like him."

I ignored the irrelevancy and waited. We were conversing, he and I, intelligently. The suspicion that trademarked his character had fled. He seemed almost pleasant, even jovial.

"How old is the carving, Mr. Ten Brink? Older than you?"

Our relationship dissolved before my eyes. Suspicion descended, and so did the V.

"Why do you want to know?" he asked me in a cold voice.

"I-I-I'm just c-curious. My dad s-says I can't just wonder about things all my life. H-h-he says I have to get answers."

A flicker of sympathy seemed to warm his ice-blue eyes, as if in that space of a breath he understood. A nice, normal sympathy for a curious fourteen-year-old. It vanished by the time I took another breath.

He pulled his gaze away from me in a jerk and stared at the floor. He didn't seem very happy for someone who got back a missing prize possession. Maybe he was ticked because he lost it in the first place and had to part with five hundred bucks' reward.

"That's a lot of money to dole out," I said. At least *I* sympathized with *him*.

Hoping I would leave, he picked up a sheaf of papers and stuffed them in his briefcase. "What money?" he said in a vague sort of way.

An odd thing to say. He had a gaping hole in his check-book and couldn't remember.

"The *reward* money."

"Reward money," he replied rather stupidly, still not getting it. Then his face came alive in remembrance.

"Oh, the *reward* money," he said.

Something triggered in me. A crazy inkling.

"I'll bet the girl who found it was pretty proud."

"Er, yes, she was. She was very proud. The reward money and all. Listen, Miss DeWinter, I have a lot of papers to grade, so I think you should—"

"A person could do a lot with five hundred dollars," I babbled on. "Buy a CD player, or Super Spectacular Nintendo. My brother loves Nintendo. Most boys do. In fact, I'll bet that's just what the kid will do with the reward."

"Hmm?"

"The boy who found your carving."

"He didn't say. Now if you please, I—"

"He or she?" I now asked in a very sly tone. He had danced right into my trap. A stupid one, but I had caught him.

He got my drift. Very slowly he turned away from his papers to look at me.

He had virtually admitted that no one had come to claim the reward and the carving was still lost. Before I could press this fascinating turn of events, Mr. Ten Brink shot out of his chair and towered menacingly over me. I didn't feel so smart now.

I clutched my textbooks to my chest and shrank back a few steps, so terrified I could have melted into the floor.

"Forget about da carrrving, okay?" he growled between his teeth. His accent kicked into high gear. He rolled his r's ferociously. "I shoulda neverrr brrought da ting here. It's found, okay? So forget already!"

I finally did what I should have done at the start. I turned tail and ran.

▪ ▪ ▪

Through the hallway, around the corner, past the doors, down the steps, I didn't stop running. I slowed to a walk only when I was three blocks away.

Since I'd missed the bus, I had plenty of time to think before I got home.

It didn't make sense. I knew he'd lied about the carving. No one had found it. At least, no one turned it in. But why? I stared down at the rumpled list of questions I still clutched.

1. *When was the last time you saw the carving?*
2. *Who were you with?*
3. *Did anyone seem too interested?*
4. *What is it worth (money-wise)?*
5. *What is it worth to you (possession-wise)?*
6. *Who made the carving?*
7. *Why did the person make a shepherd boy, as opposed to, like, a shepherd girl or even a sheep?*
8. *What does it look like?*
9. *Why did you bring it to school?*
10. *Does it have any secret compartments?*

I crumpled the paper into a tight ball and threw it to the ground. I walked a few steps, stopped, then went back and retrieved the list and shoved it into the pocket of my jeans.

I felt cold inside. Something wasn't right. Something happened back there I couldn't understand. I settled my brain down to analyze this thing from a third-party view.

Girl goes into classroom to see teacher. Teacher is . . . distracted . . . sad.

I almost stopped walking when I considered this. That's right! He wasn't just grading papers. He looked depressed. But I was so nervous, I didn't notice. I continued my review.

Teacher is staring at a paper, but his eyes aren't moving back and forth, so the girl knows he isn't reading it. Girl is intrigued by teacher's strange mood and doesn't say anything right away. Teacher makes a smart-aleck comment, and the conversation begins. The unusually perceptive girl gets a gut feeling, around the "reward" part of the conversation, that the carving wasn't turned in.

I stopped my review again to ask, why, why, why? It was bad enough to be plagued with an avalanche of curiosity, but who could take this kind of mystery? Not only did I have zero answers about the carving, but I now had the nasty feeling the carving hadn't been found and returned to Mr. Ten Brink, and he was covering it up. I shook my head. I was getting ahead of my analysis.

Girl nails teacher in lie; teacher gets irate, which proves out the lie. Girl nearly faints . . . Scratch that. Girl takes it like a trooper and turns to leave. But not before a funny feeling nearly causes her to stay and

ask more questions. Because Mr. Ten Brink is afraid.
And the girl always roots for the underdog.

Another revelation. Sure, Mr. Ten Brink was mad. He stood so close to me, I could smell his bad breath and see his eyes burn. But something else in those angry eyes sent me a message. Fear. I knew it instantly. My dad had the same kind of look when he'd come home some nights, a long time ago, when he used to work for the Mob.

I hate to see people afraid, especially older people who aren't *supposed* to be afraid. Something sure rattled Mr. Ten Brink's cage, and the carving lay at the heart of it.

I had to know more. But that meant one thing: another after-school trip to a classroom with an ornery teacher. What other option did I have? I groaned.

Talk about a fate worse than the smell of cooked liver.

Chapter Three

■

WHAT DO YOU WANT ME TO DO?" JACKIE D'AMICO WHISPERED.

"Just make sure there's no bloodshed."

For the second time in two days, I stood outside Mr. Ten Brink's classroom looking for answers. This time I had an ally. Or maybe a witness to the untimely death of a promising fourteen-year-old.

"I can't believe you're doing this," Jackie said, still whispering. "You've got guts."

"Ha! Look who's talking. Esther Z. worships the ground you walk on."

She shrugged. "That was nothing."

"You'd rather face Katie than Mr. Ten Brink?"

"In a holiday minute."

That didn't make me feel any better. "You're supposed to be here for moral support."

"I am. And to prevent bloodshed, remember?"

While Jackie and I had burned biscuits in home ec, I filled her in on the classified ad and yesterday's episode with Mr. Ten Brink. She had rewarded me with genuine interest and asked some questions of which I heartily approved. Not that I had any answers, but it was about time someone else recognized a worthy mystery.

Now I closed my eyes as I psyched myself up to go in. My lips moved as I practiced a few opening lines. "Hi, Mr. Ten Brink, remember me? You say you apologize for the crummy way you treated me yesterday? No problem. Now let's get down to business. My associate and I are here to inquire about a carving . . ."

Ready to square my shoulders and march in, I heard Jackie gulp a lungful of air. My eyes flew open and there, towering over us, stood old Cotton Swab himself. His hair looked even whiter with his dark glasses shoved up on his head.

He pulled down the glasses and stared at the two of us plastered against the lockers.

"I thought I heard something out here. Hello again, Miss DeWinter," Mr. Ten Brink said coldly. He nodded once at Jackie.

"Hi," I wheezed.

"Why are you here?" he asked, though the look on his face said he knew perfectly well why I was here.

My rehearsed speech bailed out on me. I couldn't remember a word. So I did what I do best; I blurted.

"The carving . . . I—I know it wasn't turned in. I—we want to help. It means a lot to you, and it must be found."

He fixed me with a stare that would have sent the Terminator running. The ice-blue eyes held mine for a few more seconds, then looked away. The proud shoulders came down a few inches. Before my eyes, he deflated from a tall, zealous teacher with an attitude to a stooped old man.

He looked back at me. "You remind me of someone," he said in a tone that could be mistaken for gentle.

I took a stab at it. "The person who carved the shepherd boy?"

He nodded. Then he gestured with a motion of his head

to the classroom and shuffled in. Jackie and I exchanged looks and followed him.

I'm not sure what destiny is, it sounds so mysterious, but I had a funny feeling as Jackie and I took our seats in the front-row desks and Mr. Ten Brink sat at his own. I had this definite, almost scary feeling I was in the exact place I was supposed to be at that exact minute.

Mr. Ten Brink pulled off his glasses. He polished them with his tie, then put them back on and began a story over fifty years old.

■ ■ ■

Amsterdam, Holland. May 1943.

His clothing didn't give him away. Neither did his wasted frame or gray complexion. His eyes betrayed him. Not that he fearfully looked around. He sat so still, in fact, that it was at least ten minutes into the train ride before Gerrit Ten Brink even noticed him. And when he did, he had only to see those eyes to know who this child was—and where he came from.

Gerrit had to act fast, but as discreetly as possible. He looked at his watch. Four minutes until the next stop. His heart rate jumped to a steady hammer as he sent a casual glance around the coach. Six people he recognized as the daily commuters with whom he shared the same schedule. But the gentleman at the rear of the coach and the woman seated behind him—he had never seen them before. Were they National Socialistic Bonders—traitors who would turn in their own grandmothers? Or—

Nazis.

Gerrit sat straighter and used up a precious minute to appear more interested in the scenery on the other side of the train. He finally picked up his briefcase and, not taking his eyes off the flashing landscape, crossed the aisle and slid into a seat. He now sat opposite the child, but he didn't dare look at him yet. Orange-tiled rooftops sped by.

He didn't have time to speculate about what Rene would say. He'd brought home strays before. They just never happened to be human. He looked at his watch. Two more minutes.

He caught the eye of the woman behind the seat he'd just vacated. She glanced at him, then at the child, then back to him. She knew.

Gerrit froze as fear gripped his stomach. The train began to decelerate, and passengers stirred to gather their belongings. He had no choice but to ignore the woman and no plan except to simply walk off the train with the child. Time was up. He raised his eyes to meet the face of the boy but was unprepared for what he saw. Gerrit's breath convulsed.

Misery stared out from the dark brown eyes. The child sat as limp as an unstrung marionette; his head rested back on the seat, his hands slack in his lap. His eyes returned Gerrit's gaze, but only because Gerrit happened to be in his line of vision. For a horrified second Gerrit wondered if the boy was dead. But then he knew, and the chilling thought grieved him to the point of believing that perhaps the child was better off dead, for seated before him was a child without hope.

A child without hope.

Without hope.

A sudden commotion jerked Gerrit's glance to the right. The unknown woman had spilled her valise in the center aisle and loudly berated herself for such a clumsy act.

"Oh, oh, what have I done? And all my lingerie for all the world to see! Such a disgrace!"

A few leaped to her aid, while others leaned forward to sneak a peek at the lingerie. Gerrit didn't lose a second. He leaned forward and whispered into the boy's ear, "You must trust me. I am on your side." He gently picked the child up and grabbed his briefcase.

"My humiliation is complete!" the woman wailed.

A bead of sweat trickled down from under his fedora as Gerrit slipped into the aisle just in front of the jumbled mess and headed for the door with slow, deliberate steps. He compensated against the rocking motion of the slowing train by grabbing the back of the next seat in front of him, pausing, taking a step, grabbing the next seat. His pounding heart thundered in his ears.

He reached the door and halted and didn't dare look behind him. The train rumbled and steamed to a stop.

"Why, is that my *girdle* under there?"

Gerrit grabbed the bar to the sliding door and shoved it down, then swung the door aside and stepped down to the platform. He paused a moment to shift the weight of the child. It was then that two frail arms reached up and encircled his neck; with a tiny sigh, the child rested his head on Gerrit's shoulders.

Gerrit swallowed hard and followed the stream of disembarking passengers without looking back.

■ ■ ■

Mr. Ten Brink had stopped talking. He forgot we were in the room, I think. He was somewhere back in World War II, in a faraway place called the Old Country. The Netherlands. I shuffled in my seat, then coughed.

"Where was I?"

I opened my mouth to answer, but Jackie did instead.

"Your uncle just got off the train with the little boy in his arms," she said quickly.

I turned to look at her. I was so caught up in the story, I'd forgotten she sat next to me. The intent expression on her face made me realize the carving wasn't *my* quest anymore. I turned back to Mr. Ten Brink, glad Jackie D'Amico had come to Beverly High School.

The old man picked up a paperweight, a round glass thing with swirls of color in it. He ran his hand over its surface, then set it back down and resumed his story.

■ ■ ■

Gerrit and Rene sat at the kitchen table, both more intent on the conversation in the other room than their own. Their granddaughter Katrina, barely four years old and happily oblivious to the indifference in her newfound friend, took it upon herself to show the boy proper hospitality.

"See dis?" they heard Katrina explain. "Dis is Anna, and she is mine. Anna is good, but sometimes I say, 'no no' to my Anna. She is naughty sometimes. I like to draw. I make pichers. Do you make pichers? My papa reads books. See dis? Dis is my best book. You like books?"

Fortunately, Katrina didn't seem to expect an answer and prattled on contentedly. Gerrit and Rene listened hard for a response, but none came.

Gerrit studied his wife as she concentrated on Katrina's monologue.

She had not been surprised when Gerrit stepped into the little brick home with a child in his arms. She reached for the boy and took him to the kitchen, wasting no time to get something—anything—into him. She set the child in a chair at the table, then brought water to boil and steeped overused tea leaves. Liquid was most important. She knew he probably wouldn't eat.

Gerrit leaned against the kitchen doorway and fought

tears as he watched his wife speak gently to the child. She sweetened the tea with a precious lump of sugar.

"So. I am so happy to have a visitor. And such a big boy you are! Your papa must be tall."

The child sat as weakly in the chair as he had in the train seat. But this time the dark eyes focused; he followed Rene's movements in the tiny kitchen.

She sat next to him and lifted a spoonful of tea to his lips. He didn't refuse the warm liquid but couldn't swallow the first few tries. Tea dribbled out the side of his mouth and down his chin.

"You got your eyes from your mother, I'll bet. Such beautiful eyes! A handsome boy you are. Why, in a few years the young ladies shall demand your attention."

The dribbling stopped as the boy held a spoonful of tea in his mouth, then swallowed. In ten minutes the tea cup was empty.

"So. Good for now. In a little bit we'll have more tea and some nice rye bread I made just this afternoon, eh? Now off you go to the sitting room. My grandbaby Katrina will be up from her nap in a minute, and she'll want you all to herself."

Gerrit stepped forward, picked the child up, and brought him to the couch. He settled him in a corner and propped some pillows at his side. The boy looked at him for the first time. Gerrit smiled and ruffled the filthy hair, then turned back to the kitchen.

Rene stood at the sink with her back to him. She didn't move for a very long time.

"He weighs as much as Katrina," he heard her whisper, "but he must be ten years old."

"I found him on the train," Gerrit whispered back with a glance over his shoulder.

"Did anyone see you?"

"A woman. She helped me."

"Gerrit . . . what will we do?"

■ ■ ■

Katrina awoke from her nap to find a visitor sleeping on the couch. She shook him awake before her grandparents could stop her. After a late-afternoon snack of weak tea and rye bread without butter, Katrina and her newfound friend stayed in the sitting room while Gerrit and Rene discussed the future of the silent little stranger.

"At least he ate a few bites of bread," Rene said with relief.

"I wonder when he had homemade bread last."

They listened to Katrina sing to the boy a song she'd recently learned.

"I wish he could stay," Rene said in a small voice.

Gerrit shook his head and sighed wearily.

"You know it's not possible. I'm watched even closer than ever."

"We could get another ration card perhaps. Somewhere, somehow . . ." Her voice trailed off.

"Not without further risk, Rene. I'm sorry. If we allow the boy to stay, he will not be safe. I only took him out of immediate danger."

"Then where . . . ?"

"My brother perhaps. North, in the country. Away from Amsterdam. To Andijk."

"Hans," a voice rasped, scratchy with underuse.

Gerrit and Rene froze.

"That's a nice name," Katrina said politely. "What's your last name?"

"VanderWeide."

■ ■ ■

I became aware that Mr. Ten Brink had stopped talking when I heard the clock ticking above the classroom door. The storytelling light left the teacher's eyes as he suddenly began to gather papers and shove them into his briefcase.

"It is getting late, young ladies. You must go, and I must go."

He couldn't do this.

"But—but, Mr. Ten Brink, what about the carv—"

"The time, Casey." I noticed he dropped the "Miss DeWinter."

"Yeah, but—"

"If you want to hear the rest, see me after school tomorrow."

Jackie and I reluctantly rose and started for the door. I paused at Mr. Ten Brink's desk, but he didn't even look up from his paper shuffling. Didn't even say good-bye. *Fine*, I thought angrily. *Maybe I won't even show up tomorrow. I have better things to do than spend my life—*

"Just tell me one thing," I asked, interrupting my own thoughts.

He looked up from his papers with a less-than-tolerant expression.

"Did Hans carve the shepherd boy?"

Mr. Ten Brink sure knows how to unnerve a person. He just stared at me with those frosty blue eyes. But even as he eyed me like that, I imagined a future analysis:

Girl asks innocent question. Teacher is ticked because he wants to go home. But he doesn't fool the shrewd, street-smart girl. Because she knows him now, a little. The way he told the story—nobody could tell a story like that and not be a little bit human.

He did a good job at acting insensitive though. A very good job.

"Tomorrow" was all he said. He turned his cold eyes back to his papers.

Boom. That's it. I resisted the impulse to mock his "tomorrow"—a nasty habit I've picked up from Tony.

After all my inquiries, I got nothing but rudeness. Maybe it wasn't worth it. Maybe I'd just let the old man stew in his war-story memories. Forget the stupid carving—and its owner.

I haughtily turned from the desk and strode to the classroom door where Jackie waited.

But I wasn't too far away to hear a soft voice behind me say, "Hans carved it. For me."

Chapter
Four

■

I DIDN'T SAY MUCH AS I HELPED MOM SET THE TABLE THAT EVENING. I thought about Hans VanderWeide, the boy Mr. Ten Brink so vividly described. I could picture him—dark, haunting eyes (Mr. Ten Brink didn't say "haunting," but it seemed to fit), dark hair, gaunt frame.

He hadn't explained who this child was, though I figured, despite the Dutch-sounding last name, he was Jewish.

"You've been getting home rather late from school, Casey," Mom commented. "Anything I should know about?"

"Yeah. I had to stay late to finish a few drug deals. One guy hasn't paid up, so I measured him for cement shoes."

Mom laughed. I love to make her laugh.

"You wise guy. By the way, set another plate. Marty's coming over for dinner. And make the salad please."

"Who invited him?"

She set down some glasses and looked at me. "I did. Dave and Julie are going out tonight, and they got a sitter for Kara. You don't sound too enthused."

I shrugged and continued to lay down the silverware. I inhaled appreciatively. Lasagna and garlic bread. I should have guessed. Marty dies over my mom's lasagna, so she fixes it whenever he's over. Which used to be once a week.

Mom and Dad have been friends with Marty's parents since before we were born. Julie is my mom's best friend, so Marty and I, only two months apart, grew up like a brother and sister. We did everything together. In the last year, our first year of high school, things have been different. He has basketball and baseball and the paper route he took over for his older brother, who went to college. I have softball and school plays. And I read a lot, which has always been a source of irritation to Marty. More than once I've been coaxed against my will out of a mystery or adventure book to go poke around in the woods with Marty, looking for a place to build yet another fort.

So things have changed. That's cool with me, because we're too busy to notice, though I miss him when I think about it. We still call ourselves best friends, if only from stubbornness. But best friends do stuff together—like investigate strange classified ads.

I hate to make salads. Why not just eat a raw carrot and call it good? Wash the lettuce, dry it out, chop up celery and green pepper and carrots and cucumbers and radishes and green onions and tomatoes, throw the whole mess in a bowl, then clean up all the celery, green pepper, carrot, cucumber, radish, green onion, tomato leaves, seeds, and clingy scrapings. Exhausted by the time I put the salad bowl on the table, I snuck a chocolate-chip cookie and went to my room to wait for dinner.

I lay on my bed and munched while I stared at the ceiling.

So Gerrit Ten Brink was Mr. Ten Brink's uncle. Wow. He was actually alive during World War II, living in that funny sounding city. Ondyke?

Before Mr. Ten Brink got to the part where Gerrit found Hans on the train, he told us about the condition of his country in 1943. Hitler's army invaded the Netherlands on May 10, 1940. It started when they bombed Rotterdam, a city on the ocean. Holland surrendered in only five days.

"We would wake up in the middle of the night to hear planes overhead," Mr. Ten Brink had said with that back-in-the-Old-Country look on his face. "They were heading east from England to bomb war factories in Germany—though sometimes we wondered if they were German planes ready to wipe us out like Rotterdam."

I've had my share of living in fear, back when my dad worked for a gangster. No kidding! He worked for the local Mob, sort of against his will, until he got out of it and became a Christian and—well, more about that later. My point is, I know what it's like to be scared, but not the kind of fear where I'd wonder if a warplane would drop a bomb on my house.

Mr. Ten Brink spoke of ration cards—books with weekly coupons in them. Each person got one ration card from city hall. The coupons were good for whatever commodity was on hand that week. Many times basic stuff like sugar, meat, and butter was not available. His mother sometimes cooked tulip bulbs from the garden to eat.

"Casey!" Tony bellowed. "Time for dinner!"

■ ■ ■

I was glad Marty came to dinner, if only because I hadn't had lasagna in a long time. My dad served me up a second helping as I reached for more garlic bread.

"Your mother says you've taken up a new occupation after school," Dad said with a smile in his eyes.

Marty stared at me. "You working for the new McDonald's?"

"Nope. I'm selling drugs."

"Oh. Could you pass the French dressing?"

I studied Marty while I handed him the dressing. Bright red hair the color of the dressing rambled in every direction. Freckles sprinkled his nose and cheeks, left over from the summer. He had a splotch of sauce on his chin.

Marty has the most beautiful eyes I've ever seen. Crystal-clear, gray-green. Long lashes. Guys shouldn't be allowed to have lashes like that, I've often lamented. Mine are short and skimpy, though I refuse to wear mascara yet.

I've noticed some of the girls at school noticing him. I don't know if I'm jealous or not. Certainly not in a boyfriend/girlfriend way, but maybe in a best friend way.

A comment from Tony jolted my thoughts away from Marty. "She's playing private investigator and bugging Mr. Ten Brink about the classified ad," I heard my annoying brother say.

I glared at him. How did he know? He had his football and homework and girlfriends. What did he care?

"What classified ad?" Dad asked.

I couldn't resist. I jumped up and ran to get my mythology book and brought the ad back to Dad. He read it and handed it to Mom.

"Well, that sounds very interesting. What did you find out from Mr. Ten Brink? Did anyone find it yet?"

All eyes were on me. Marty and Tony both looked up from their plates with sincere interest. But I felt funny all of a sudden. I'd have to explain my catching Mr. Ten Brink in a lie and that after two days of after-school inquiries I really didn't know anything about the carving . . . except who carved it.

"So who carved it, Case?" Tony asked.

I looked at my big brother and smiled against my will. So, while we lingered over the last of the lasagna and strawberry shortcake for dessert, I told them everything. We sat in silence for a while after we finished. Thinking about a skinny Jewish kid.

As Marty left for home that night, he stopped with his hand on the doorknob and said over his shoulder, "Uh, mind if I come with you to Mr. Ten Brink's class?"

I shrugged as I smiled at my best friend. "Sure. Jackie was with me today. I don't think Mr. Ten Brink will mind another."

"Cool. See ya."

"See ya."

■ ■ ■

Marty wasn't the only one to join Jackie and me at what had become our after-school ritual. In the third row back, looking as bored as I must look in my geometry class, sat Anthony Edward DeWinter. He wanted to surprise me—and he did. He about made me choke on my gum, but I refused to let him know it. I nodded to him coolly and took my front-row seat next to Jackie. Marty joined Tony.

Mr. Ten Brink didn't appear surprised in the least at Tony's presence, which surprised me, but he did eye Marty as he came into the room with a cup of coffee. He seemed uncomfortable, and I felt more than a little guilty. After all, Mr. Ten Brink was covering something up—the shepherd boy hadn't been turned in, but the search was called off—and I was bringing more and more people into this thing.

"I hope you don't mind, Mr. Ten Brink—" I said sheepishly. "I read the ad to Marty a few days ago and—"

Mr. Ten Brink waved me to silence. "It is a worthy story. I am proud of my family, proud of my heritage. You do me honor to listen."

Well, color me shocked. That was the first personal

thing Mr. Ten Brink ever said to me, in front of God and everybody. I felt my cheeks grow warm and suppressed a foolish smile.

■ ■ ■

Andijk, the Netherlands. June 1943.

Four weeks in the care of Rene Ten Brink put twelve pounds on Hans VanderWeide's thin body. Good broth and tea accounted for most of the weight, since the child had arrived severely dehydrated.

Katrina threw a raging fit the day Gerrit took Hans away. She clung to him and cried and refused to let him leave. Hans knelt, held the little shoulders, and looked into Katrina's tear-stained face.

"But if you come with me, little one, who will take care of Oma Rene?"

Katrina blinked in surprise. Opa had to take Hans away, up in the country where she had never been. Who *would* watch over Oma? She must protect Oma from the men in the brown clothes. The ones Oma and Opa were so afraid of.

"I will," she said, still crying. "I will take care of Oma."

Hans turned to Rene.

"My mama prays for someone like you—to help her son."

Rene nodded. The motion shook down a few tears from her brimming eyes. She held out her arms, gathered in Hans, and stroked his soft, clean hair. She kissed his cheek, then stood back to look at him for a long moment.

"I will worry about you. Be a good boy."

"I will, Oma. I will see you again someday."

She nodded, then made a shooing motion. "So catch your train already. And memorize the names of your new relatives."

Hans smiled. "I already did."

■ ■ ■

Gerrit glanced at Hans, leaning against the window fast asleep. The last time he'd seen Hans on a train, he thought the boy to be dead. A child without hope.

He smiled now, though his smile faded quickly. What did the future hold for the boy? For the Netherlands? How long would the Germans occupy their land? How many more would die before their own flag flew from The Hague once more? Would it ever?

He remembered when he enjoyed day trips like this. A time when he didn't cast furtive glances at others who cast furtive glances at him. A time when he didn't finger the precious identification papers inside his blazer, papers he'd had to produce more than once to suspicious German officers. Officers who, at mood or whim, could detect a flaw in the impeccable papers and have him sent away.

He looked again at the boy, and his stomach surged with anxiety. Travel alone was fearful enough; with a Jewish boy, it was terrifying.

The forged ID papers for Hans took two weeks to obtain. Gerrit chose carefully whom to bribe, and then only on a good tip. Rene's silver candlesticks had to be sold, since their survival had eaten the savings account long ago.

The day Gerrit found Hans, he knew the boy to be Jewish. He learned later that he was also the son of one of the highest-ranking officials in the country, a governor advisor to one of the eleven provinces. The new ID papers Gerrit carried for Hans told a different story. Now the VanderWeide boy was a humble Ten Brink: Kees Wilhelm Ten Brink.

Position meant nothing now. Being Jewish meant death.

■ ■ ■

The train took them as far as Hoorn, where a man with a pony and cart waited. He brought them to Lutjebroek and waved good-bye while they began the last few miles on foot to Andijk.

Dusty and tired, but glad to see the town of his youth once more, Gerrit picked up the pace as they reached the outskirts of Andijk.

The town was a tulip community, one of the nation's highest exporters of the beautiful Dutch bulbs. The fields of Andijk merrily mocked Hitler's war. Vibrant colors rang out beauty; the flowers bloomed gloriously, oblivious to the nation's heartache. Gerrit and Hans stopped at the first flower crop and stared in awe.

"Enjoy it," a grim voice informed them. "'Tis the last of them we shall see for heaven knows how long."

An old woman stood at Gerrit's side and looked upon the same field with grieving eyes.

"We cook the bulbs to eat," she said bitterly. She turned away before they could reply.

Gerrit sighed. He fixed a stare on the brilliant field. He wanted to remember Holland as it once was. This blaze of glory.

As they continued through the town, Gerrit's shoulders came up even straighter. He set his lips in a firm line. Holland's strength had buckled beneath the weight of its conquerors three years earlier, but Holland's spirit would never surrender.

A Jewish boy walked beside him. Proof enough.

■ ■ ■

"The boy we knew as Kees stayed with our family for almost two years," the teacher said. "During that time he and I became brothers. We trapped fish, built hideouts, even threw firecrackers at German jeeps. All this time, only Papa and Mama knew who he really was. Myself and my five sisters knew him only as Cousin Kees."

He broke off to take a sip of what I'm sure was cold coffee.

"The war ended a few months after he left. But my parents kept silent about Kees's identity. It wasn't until I begged to visit Kees in Amsterdam that they finally told me. Told me that Kees wasn't another city boy sent to the country to fatten up, as happened commonly throughout the war.

"Hans and his mother and father had been arrested shortly after the Germans invaded Holland. To them the VanderWeides were doubly guilty: they were Jewish, and Jamil VanderWeide (Hans's father) was a government official. They were sent to a labor camp in Holland, a place called Vught. After many months Hans decided to escape, to try to find his older brother who had joined the Allied armies. His plan, the brave dream of a ten-year-old, was to bring his brother back and together they would rescue their parents.

"For weeks Hans worked to dig a hole beneath a barbed-wire fence and one day made his escape. He wandered like a tramp for a long while, unable to find his way back home, not knowing where to look for his brother. Miraculously, he wasn't arrested by the Nazis or turned in by suspicious National Socialistic Bonders."

"What happened to his parents?" Jackie asked.

"They were sent to a concentration camp in Poland not long after Hans escaped."

My shoulders slumped. I've read enough history to know that millions of people who went to the concentration camps in World War II did not come out alive.

"Jamil and Naomi VanderWeide were gassed," Mr. Ten Brink said quietly. "The last memory Hans had of his mother was of her pushing a wheelbarrow full of stone from a rock pile."

The brave dream of a ten-year-old. I felt tears sting my eyes but held them back desperately. No way would I cry in front of everybody.

Mr. Ten Brink continued, his voice quiet. "I cried for my friend when Papa told me. Cried for his mama and papa. Cried because I was angry Hans never told me. But Papa pulled me on his lap and held me, though I was a big boy of thirteen, and said Hans didn't tell me because he loved me. He loved all of us. The more we knew about him, the more danger we'd be in.

"Uncle Gerrit found Hans's brother and made arrangements through the Underground to get Kees safely to England. The day he left, I thought he was going back to Amsterdam."

▪ ▪ ▪

Andijk, the Netherlands. February 1945.

Kees and Johann slipped away from their chores early. Later that day Uncle Gerrit would come for Kees. They were willing to risk a whipping if Papa discovered the undone chores.

They tramped across damp fields to their favorite fort, a semi-underground cave dug into the side of a small knoll. They pulled back the bound flap of thatch used to cover their entrance and dropped down into the hole.

Pilfered smoking materials, a few grubby cherry bombs, glass marbles, and a dog-eared deck of cards missing the two of spades were cached in cubbyholes throughout the tiny hideout. But neither felt like doing much of anything. They sat next to each other with knees drawn up and backs against the cold earthen wall.

Johann looked sideways at his friend and thought about

the first day he saw Kees. Skinny, white as Mama's curtains, quiet and shy. Now he probably weighed more than Johann. He couldn't believe he ever thought of Kees as shy.

"What are you looking at?" Kees growled in a great imitation of Mr. Klaas, the neighbor nearest to the Ten Brinks.

Johann smiled, but he wasn't in the mood for joking around. In a little while Uncle Gerrit would come. He didn't want Kees to go.

"The war isn't even over yet. Why can't you stay longer?" he asked Kees for the fifth time.

"I don't know," Kees answered, dropping the playful tone. "My mama and papa probably miss me. I miss them."

"But they didn't even write to you."

Kees ignored this. A twinkle came into his dark eyes again.

"I have something for you." He crawled to the end of the hole, then came back with something wrapped in a piece of dirty brown leather. He handed it to Johann.

Johann held it for a moment. "I didn't get you anything," he said doubtfully.

"I didn't *get* you this either. I *made* it. Now open it, Noodle-brain."

When Johann pulled off the leather wrapping, he held in his hand a small wooden carving of a boy with a lamb draped across his shoulders. A pouch was slung over his arm and fell to the boy's hip. The lad held the feet of the lamb, and a smile played on his wooden lips.

Though it was a rough carving, not polished or smooth, Johann held his breath at the beauty of the thing. He stared at his friend, amazed he had kept this talent hidden so long.

"It's a shepherd," Kees said with a small, self-conscious shrug.

"Kees . . . it's . . . it's beautiful."

"I don't know about *beautiful*."

"I've never seen anything like it. Why didn't you tell me you could carve like this?"

"I wanted to surprise you. My papa taught me how. He was a part-time carpenter."

Johann turned it around in his hands. "I'll keep it forever. I mean it. Forever. You can teach me how to carve when I visit you someday—or when you come back to visit us."

Kees nodded. "You know why it's a shepherd, don't you?"

Johann hesitated. It was a strange subject with them.

When Kees first came to Andijk, Johann had a hard time understanding Kees's fascination with the little church the family attended. He had stared around at everything, absorbed the sermons like he'd never heard such talk. He chatted at length with a delighted Mama on stuff Johann felt should be discussed at church only.

Johann finally confronted Kees with his concerns.

"Kees," he had said after Kees had a lively discussion with the church minister, "you act like you've never gone to church before."

"I never have," Kees truthfully answered.

Johann couldn't believe it. *A Ten Brink not go to church?* It must be some strange branch of the family Kees came from.

"I don't see what the big deal is," Johann had said with an impatient gesture at the minister.

Kees answered with shining eyes, "Johann, do you realize that Jesus was *Jewish*?"

"He was not. He was a Christian."

"But He was Jewish too."

Johann couldn't answer because he failed to see what difference that made.

"Do you know that if He lived on earth right now, this very

instant, He would be sent to the camps for being a Jew? Imagine! They'd send away His mother and all His family. Even His friends. They'd wreck His carpenter business, smash it all up, and probably burn it."

"They wouldn't do that to Him," Johann snapped. "I wouldn't let them."

"Neither would I."

Each boy considered this in silence. Then a thought occurred to Johann.

"Hey, Kees, did you know that the guys who put Jesus to death were Jewish?"

Kees's face darkened. "Yeah, I know. They call—they call them Christ killers. I don't get that part."

"Neither do I."

Kees suddenly brightened. "But the minister said that the Roman soldiers actually put Him on the cross—not the Jews."

"Oh, yeah!"

Johann decided to let Kees in on a secret, since they were on the subject. He looked over his shoulders and all around, then leaned conspiratorially toward Kees.

"Mum's the word," he said out of the side of his mouth, "but my best friend Willem's dad once hid a Jew in their back shed for a whole week."

Kees's eyes widened. "No kidding?"

"No kidding. Had him right under stinking Nazi noses."

Now Johann stared at the shepherd boy.

"Yeah, I know why you made it."

Kees smiled. "Because Jesus said He was a shepherd who gave His life for the sheep. And He was a *Jew.* I found that out here."

"Your dad must be some part-time carpenter to teach you to carve like this."

"He is," Kees answered proudly, "and I'm going to see him again."

"Of course you are," Johann groused dismally. "Uncle Gerrit should be here anytime."

Johann rewrapped the carving and stuffed it inside his shirt. They crawled out of the shelter and replaced the thatch, then started back to the house.

The westering sun made beautiful colors in the evening sky. The boys walked toward it silently, hands stuffed in pockets. Uncle Gerrit waited at the gate with Papa.

With one hand on the carving inside his shirt, Johann waved good-bye to Kees. He never saw him again.

Chapter Five

■

WHAT DO YOU MEAN YOU NEVER SAW HANS AGAIN?" I DIDN'T
mean for my voice to crack.

"Was he caught?" Jackie asked.

"Sent to the gas chambers?" Marty demanded to know.

"What about Uncle Gerrit?" Tony inquired.

Mr. Ten Brink smiled at the flurry of responses. I didn't
see anything to smile about. I wanted to throttle him! Hans
could be dead!

"My uncle lived to the ripe old age of ninety-three. He
helped three more Jews after Hans."

"*What about Hans?*"

"Hans escaped to England."

I shook my head and said insistently, "But you said you
never saw Hans again."

"I never have."

"But he's written to you."

"No. Haven't had any contact with him since 1945."

"What!" I exploded. "But you guys saved his life! You and
he were like brothers! He never tried to thank you or even see
how you were doing?"

The teacher shook his head and started to say something.

"What an ingrate!" I ranted.

"Casey . . ." Mr. Ten Brink began softly.

"What a thankless—" Anger robbed me of eloquence. "—noodle-brain!"

"Casey . . ."

"Of all the nerve—"

"Casey!"

I closed my mouth and blinked at him. He glared at me with a strange expression, then sighed and looked at the others. As he got up to go to the classroom door, he rubbed his hand over his face and I could hear him muttering.

We watched as Mr. Ten Brink poked his head out the door and looked in both directions. Satisfied, he turned back into the room and closed the door behind him. Then he went to the windows and looked out of each one. He twisted the venetian blinds shut. We stared at each other, perplexed.

He walked back to his desk but didn't sit at his chair. He half-sat on the front of the desk. He motioned for Tony and Marty to come up to the front seats.

"I don't know why I tell you this," he said in a voice just above a whisper. "Others have come to help me look for the carving. But you are different." He threw a look in my direction. An irritated look, I thought.

"I have only told you the first half of the story, how the carving came to be. The next half is—well, it has me confounded to say the least. A few weeks ago I received a letter from, of all places, Jerusalem, Israel. From a place called Yad Vashem."

"I've heard of that place," Tony said. "Isn't that some kind of memorial for the Jews? For the Jews killed in the Holocaust?"

Mr. Ten Brink nodded, and then the history teacher in him came out in full force. He got lecturish.

"It's west of Jerusalem, on a hill called the Mount of Remembrance. 'Yad Vashem' is Hebrew that translated means 'name and place.' The names of the murdered Jews are recorded in a repository called the Hall of Names. Last I heard, they had over three million names. The list still grows after all this time.

"Well, along the path leading to Yad Vashem from the parking lot are rows of trees, planted in honor of people who saved Jewish lives during World War II. It is called the Avenue of the Righteous. A 'place and name' is given to the hero Gentiles as well. So many carob trees have been planted, extending even past the memorial, that it actually became a beautiful grove."

"Why carob?" Marty asked.

"It's from a passage in the Bible, Psalm 1: 'Blessed is he who does not walk in the counsel of the wicked. He is like a tree planted by the streams of water, which yields its fruit in its season, and its leaf does not wither.' I believe they chose the carob tree because it has leather-like leaves that do not wither."

"Hans didn't forget," I whispered.

When everybody turned to look at me, I realized I had spoken out loud.

"What do you mean?" Tony asked in his perturbed big-brother voice.

I ignored him and looked at Mr. Ten Brink. "He didn't forget, did he? That's why you got the letter from Yad Vashem."

He didn't speak immediately, but his slow smile and the spark in his eyes told me I was right. I couldn't resist a triumphant glance at Tony.

"Hans didn't forget. I knew he'd never forget me. But that isn't really the point. Many people helped many Jews during the War. It wasn't as remarkable then as it seems today. We did what we had to do. It never surprised me that I didn't hear from Hans. Our paths met for a brief time, then parted." He paused a moment before he continued.

"The letter from Yad Vashem stated that Hans VanderWeide had placed an application in my family's name for a right to a tree at Yad Vashem." He broke off for a moment to look at each one of us. "It was one of the last things Hans did. He died of a brain aneurysm shortly after he placed the application."

That stunned me, but not nearly as much if the teacher would have said Hans had been captured by the Nazis.

"How old was he?" my brother asked quietly.

"Sixty-three."

"Wow," Marty mused, "that's about fifty-three years longer than if he woulda got caught on the train instead of found by your uncle."

Mr. Ten Brink nodded and smiled sadly. "You see the honor of my heritage? The letter from the Committee on the Righteous of Nations was a preliminary inquiry as to my identity. They had been searching for a long while. You see, there are a lot of Johann Ten Brinks in the Netherlands. Like someone named Joe Johnson in the United States. And many Ten Brinks emigrated."

"Well, I think it's great," Jackie said brightly, "that they've finally found you. Your family can be honored for saving Hans's life."

"The letter questioned the existence of a wooden carving—a carving that would help prove my identity. Hans knew I would keep it forever, so he used it as a point of reference. Something to differentiate me from the other Johann Ten Brinks in the North Holland province. The Jewish people take this investigation very seriously. Testimony is taken, witnesses and records examined. They hold this selection process to be so important that a justice of the Supreme Court of Israel chairs the Committee."

"No problem," I said. "Just cough up the carving and—"

I could have bitten off my idiot tongue. My brilliance amazes me. Even Jackie shot me a reproachful glance.

"I kind of forgot the carving is lost," I murmured meekly as I slunk down into my seat.

Mr. Ten Brink shook his head, and the weird feeling I had when I first talked with him came back in a swoop. I sat straight up. My nose tingled. (It always tingles when I either get really freaked out or when a hunch kind of feeling comes over me.)

"The carving is not lost."

I held my breath and waited for him to continue. I watched as his expression sagged and darkened. The beaten old man look. I liked the snappy teacher look better.

"One evening, two days after I got the letter, I received a phone call. The man said he was an investigator from Yad Vashem, and he wanted to see the carving. He wanted to meet me after school the following day. So I agreed. I waited and waited and was about to leave at 5:30 when the man showed up." He darted an anxious glance at the door.

"He was a tall, medium-build fellow with dark hair everywhere—even on his knuckles. Wore dark sunglasses that he didn't take off. A few gold chains around his neck, a ruby earring with little diamonds around it in one ear. His hair was slicked back into a ponytail.

"He didn't ask me any questions about Hans—or about my family. He only wanted to see the carving. So," Mr. Ten Brink said with a heavy sigh, "I gave it to him. Three days later

I got a call from a representative of the Israeli Embassy in New York. She said she was assigned to investigate the Ten Brink case for prospective recognition from Yad Vashem. She wanted to meet with me, interview me, and see the carving."

Total silence. Then we couldn't hold it in any longer.

"Holey moley!"

"Who was the buzzard breath who took the carving?"

"Why would the scumbag do such a thing?"

"How did he know you had it?"

Mr. Ten Brink shook his head at our shotgun questions. He lifted his hands in a helpless gesture and let them fall back in his lap.

"I'm as baffled as you. The carving had value only to me. Or so I thought. Hoping he would return it, I placed an ad in the paper but had them remove it after it ran only one day. The man didn't look like he needed the five hundred dollar reward."

"We'll help you find it, Mr. Ten Brink," my brother said.

"That's right."

"Absolutely."

"No!" the teacher barked.

I jumped a little.

"I—I told you the story of Hans because it is important for you to know history, to know sacrifices made. I wanted to answer Casey's question about who made the carving. That's the only reason I told you. Forget about the carving. It's not your business," he growled icily.

My earlier prognosis was right. Something had rattled his cage, and Hairy Knuckles was it.

"What about the person from the Israeli Embassy?" Marty asked. "What did you tell her?"

"I told her I wasn't interested." Mr. Ten Brink seemed to

withdraw into himself. He went around his desk and began his stuff-the-briefcase thing. I knew he wanted us to leave.

Tony motioned with his head toward the door. Each of us got up, thanked Mr. Ten Brink for his time, and departed. I left last.

I paused at the door and risked a backward glance. Mr. Ten Brink had stopped his briefcase stuffing and was staring at the venetian blinds like he could see through them. I wondered what he saw—a dark-haired boy, a carving of a shepherd, or the face of the man who took it away?

I wanted the other Mr. Ten Brink back. The one who told us about Kees/Hans, about the famous Dutch fields filled with flowers, about a place in Israel where they remembered heroes.

It's not fair!

Grinding my teeth, I shut the door and stormed down the hallway so mad I couldn't see straight.

I stomped down the steps and shoved open the door. Then I became aware of someone behind me, and I turned my head for a second.

They were *all* behind me. Tony, Jackie, and Marty. No one said a word; they just followed me. I didn't care where I was going, but I wanted to get there fast.

After four blocks I started to cool down, and my pace slowed. All three were still with me, and we walked four abreast. Marty seemed sullen, Tony thoughtful, Jackie depressed. They looked like I felt. We walked down a side street to the Hamilton Elementary School and wandered to the playground in the back.

Tony climbed to the top of the muscle bars and perched on the top rung. Jackie sat in a swing and began to idly twist herself around in it. Marty laid down on a teeter-totter board and laced his hands behind his head. I climbed up the slide ladder and sat down on the top.

I gazed at the sun's reflection off the aluminum slide until my eyes hurt.

"Well, my worthy compatriots," Marty said with his eyes closed, "what are we going to do?"

"I have no idea," Tony answered from above, "but we've got to start somewhere."

Jackie frowned and kicked a few pebbles as she turned around in the swing. "Maybe the Israeli Embassy. Maybe we could start there."

Sudden tears stung my eyes—and not because of the bright reflection.

They knew it too. A tree belonged on the Avenue of the Righteous in the Ten Brinks' name. For all of them: Gerrit, Rene, the mom and dad . . . and Johann.

"We'll find the carving or die trying," I declared. My voice echoed back from the school buildings.

And with that sentiment, a partnership formed. Jackie D'Amico, sometime champion of the downtrodden, expert second baseman for the girls softball team. Marty Behrens, class clown (or class goofball) and best friend. Tony DeWinter, football halfback and honor roll student and a decent brother. Casey DeWinter. Uh, not notably anything. Except I read the classifieds and I'm a sucker for underdogs. Even aged, grumpy ones.

Chapter
Six

■

As I brushed my teeth and got ready for bed that night, I thought about Hans. Hans the kid. But I couldn't think about him too much because my mind would blank out when I thought about how he was separated from his parents for two years, all that time thinking he'd be reunited and . . . See what I mean? Sometimes the mind *has* to blank out.

I thought about my own parents. Mom is fun. She plays board games with me when I'm, well, bored. And I don't mind being sick sometimes because she lets me set up camp in the living room surrounded by books, word search puzzle magazines, a barf bowl, and a two-liter bottle of ginger ale. There's an extra-gentle tone in her voice at such times, and usually I milk it for all I'm worth. She's on to me sometimes, though.

When I was a little girl, I thought my daddy was like all daddies. Indisputably the best, of course. I figured he did what other dads did. Went to work, brought home the bacon, played with the kids occasionally, and had a weird obsession for the TV remote control.

Dad was a tax accountant for a business in Selby, the big city twenty minutes from Hamilton. But his tax firm, Marcus, Libby and Associates, wasn't owned by Marcus or Libby. It was owned by Hernando Giminez—the Godfather.

Dad started with Marcus and Libby fresh out of college. He worked his way up from a junior clerk to a senior executive and handled all the big-time accounts from Selby: Kell Contractors, the Gannon grocery chain, Startime Video stores, and a bunch more.

I'm fuzzy on the details, but here's the gist of it: the Godfather owned Marcus and Libby. On the outside they were a respectable company. On the inside they were as rotten as a potato gone bad. (Ever get a whiff of a rotten potato? We had one once in a bushelful we got from the farmer's market. We thought something had croaked in the garage.)

Anyway, Dad had suspected something wasn't on the up and up at Marcus and Company for years, but he didn't say anything. Just did his job and kept quiet about it. Then a junior clerk came to him one day with a sheet of numbers on a flower shop in Selby. The guy couldn't figure out why the shop made so much money when he knew for a fact (he lived next door to it) that it was never busy.

Trouble was, Dad knew the Godfather owned the flower shop. The Godfather owned a lot of businesses Marcus and Company did work for. The Godfather owned, in fact, Kell Contractors and Startime Video stores. So Dad knew this junior clerk, Bixby, was on to something with the flower shop. Sure, they sold flowers. I know now that behind the scenes they also sold a few hundred thousand dollars worth of cocaine each year.

That's where all the figures on Bixby's balance sheet came from. They call it laundering money. Kind of a catchy term, laundering. See, what happens is the money received from cocaine sales is dirty, bad money. Money you can't just toss into a bank account because the bank has rules that say Joe Blow can't deposit a hundred thousand dollars without proof of where he got the money. Sales receipts from a flower shop are legit, but Joe Blow isn't going to give Uncle Sam a receipt for a cocaine sale.

So drug dealers add the dirty money to the daily sales of a legitimate business. The money is deposited in the bank under Fanny's Flower Shop and *voila*—the cash becomes clean. You learn a lot as a daughter of an ex-organized crime accountant.

Then along come guys like Graham Bixby who know for a fact that Fanny's Flower Shop is about as busy as a Popsicle stand at the North Pole. Dad tried to convince him to shut up about what he discovered and do his job without asking questions. I'll never forget the night when I was nine and was supposed to be in bed. Instead, I sat at the bottom of the stairs and listened in on the conversation in the kitchen.

Dad had come home late that night, talking louder than usual, so I knew he was drunk. But at least I could hear everything clearly.

"Just couldn't shut up, could he. Had to blow his mouth off after I told him a hundred times to let it lie. He's vanished, Maureen. Gone. Nothing left but a wedding ring."

"Shhh! Keep your voice down! Who's gone?"

"Who do you think?" Dad slurred. "Good ol' Graham Bixby. Didn't show up at the office today."

Mom sounded tired. "What happened, Phil?"

I heard the fridge open, then the pop and hiss of a can.

"He'd been missing all weekend. Lisa found his wedding ring in an envelope in the mailbox." Dad snorted. "Cops think maybe he just skipped out of town. Ha. They don't know Graham Bixby very well."

"Oh no," I barely heard Mom whisper. "Poor Lisa. How old is the baby?"

Dad didn't say anything for a minute. Then, "Seven months. Graham had seven pictures lined up on his desk for every month the kid got older."

I listened hard but didn't hear anything for a while. I remembered Graham and Lisa. They came over for dinner once when Lisa was very pregnant. She smiled a lot and smelled nice.

"What are we going to do, Phil?"

"What we've always done. If I play along, everything is fine. If I make a sound, I wind up like Bixby. Or one of my family does."

"Has that man contacted you again?" Mom asked.

"Robbie Burns? No. He got the message last time. I'm not interested."

"But maybe—"

"I said I'm not interested! Get it? He could be lying, Maureen! Maybe he's *not* undercover FBI. Maybe he's one of Giminez's men, just testing my loyalty."

"I never thought about that," Mom said quietly.

"If I make one move to cooperate with him, I'll find a present waiting in my car someday. Only I'll never know who gave it to me because I'll be vaporized."

I remembered the name Robbie Burns from another conversation I'd eavesdropped on. Supposedly this guy worked as a henchman for the Godfather. The scary loan-shark type. Only he told my dad he was actually an FBI agent, and he'd been working undercover in the Giminez racket for years. He was trying to assemble enough evidence to take down not only Hernando Giminez, but a bunch of other Mob kingpins as well—guys who did business with Giminez from all over the world.

"What if this man is who he says he is?" Mom asked.

"Then we could get out of this mess. You could trade your testimony for freedom. We could move far away, and I'd never again worry myself into ulcers every single time you or the kids leave the house. All I want is freedom, Phil!" Mom's voice got trembly. "All I want is to live without fear! Is that too much to ask?"

"Let's stick to just living, okay, Maureen?" Dad answered coldly.

▪ ▪ ▪

Funny how things turn out.

This Robbie Burns turned out to be Mr. Persistence. He'd run into my dad in the strangest places, like the waiting room at the dentist's office. While my dad waited for his appointment, Robbie filled his ears with promises of freedom from the Mob and long life for his kids. That's not all he told Dad. He told Dad about freedom of a different kind.

We had never been churchgoers. My dad was fed up with religion. He had it shoved down his throat as a kid, he always told us, and he swore he'd never do that to his own children. So my knowledge about God and the Bible was just about zero. Every Christmas Mom would set up this Nativity scene on the TV. Even though baby Jesus had a chip in His ceramic cheek, I have always regarded that particular Yuletide decoration with wonder. Maybe that counts for something.

Anyway, that's it for my religious upbringing. Oh, and we went to church every Easter with Grandpa and Grandma Dodge. But Robbie Burns, this loan shark/FBI guy, had a spin on God that went beyond Nativity scenes and Easter bonnets.

Bottom line, Dad started to change. After Graham Bixby vanished, Robbie Burns laid it on thick both in the Mob and God arenas. He said what Dad needed was not only freedom from the Mob, but freedom from fear. We started going to this little community church, Hamilton Bible Church.

It was cool. Based on Dad's experience, I really didn't want anything to do with God. Wasn't interested. But this church— the *people* at this church—made me interested.

Dad stopped drinking. Said he didn't need to. Mom smiled more often. And one certain conversation I listened to explained it all to me.

■ ■ ■

I sat in my usual place at the bottom of the stairs with my arms wrapped around my knees. Mom and Dad were in the living room. I had to be extra-quiet since the living room is closer to the stairs than the kitchen.

"When does it go to trial?" Mom asked.

"April 15th. Ironic, isn't it?" Dad laughed.

I wished I knew what *ironic* meant.

"Do you have to testify?"

"Robbie says no. The information Tim, Bruce, and I provided is evidence enough. This way, Giminez and company won't know we collaborated with the FBI. They'll think it was an outside sting operation."

"That means we won't have to relocate?"

"Exactly."

"What happens to Robbie? I mean, what about his undercover work?"

"I don't know. They're still trying to nail someone named Claudio Muhtara who had worked with Giminez on international dealings. Other FBI agents will handle the prosecution so they can keep Robbie out of it. They want Giminez. Through Giminez, maybe they can get to Muhtara. If Robbie can keep up his Mob connections, they'll have a better chance to nail

Muhtara. Remember, it's taken years for Robbie to establish himself as one of Giminez's key men. They don't want to blow that now."

"But what kind of life does Robbie have in the Mob? I mean, he's a Christian. Isn't he forced to do things that are against what he believes?"

Dad sighed. "I don't know. He once told me with a twinkle in his eye that the Lord works in mysterious ways. And He sure does. Who would have believed *I* would become a Christian, through the Mob of all things? Anyway, Robbie says he works hard to keep his cover. That's about all he says."

"I'd like to meet him someday," Mom remarked.

"Sorry to say, you probably won't. He's too smart to make any possible slip-ups like that. He couldn't let any of his Mob buddies see him with anyone who would raise suspicions."

"What about meeting with you?"

"He's an expert, and it was necessary."

They were silent a minute.

"Oh, Phil, I can't believe it's actually happening. We're going to be free. You'll have a new job soon when Marcus and Libby is out of business, and we won't even have to move. It's incredible!"

Dad laughed a happy, low chuckle that warmed me to the toes. "You know, I read a great verse the other day in Proverbs. It says, 'When a man's ways are pleasing to the Lord, he makes even his enemies live at peace with him.' I tell you, I got more than I ever bargained for when I told God I'd finally had enough—that I was sick of running away from everything, even Him."

"We still may be in for a rough ride."

"I'm not proud of what I've done—or what I didn't do. Maybe if I would have come forward sooner, Graham would still be around. That's something I'll have to live with. But *God's* with us, Maureen. I never thought I'd live in peace, but now . . ."

■ ■ ■

That was five years ago. The FBI quietly brought down Hernando Giminez and dissolved the partnership of Marcus, Libby and Associates. Robbie Burns disappeared into the Mob realm. As far as I know, Dad hasn't seen him since. Dad and the two other accountants were given immunity (that means they got off the hook for participating in criminal activity) because they cooperated with the FBI.

The few businesses Marcus and Company legitimately dealt with were transferred to a brand new tax firm— DeWinter, Grabil and Whittaker Tax and Business Service.

The real kicker for me was how Mom actually believed Tony and I had no clue about Dad's business. Like we were a couple of no-brainers who couldn't figure out things on our own. The day they sat us down to tell us everything, Tony and I had to pull off some fake surprise expressions. We could've won Oscars. "You're kidding! *Dad in the Mob?*"

They didn't tell us about Robbie. Probably didn't want to risk blowing his cover. We knew about Robbie Burns only from my midnight surveillance missions at the foot of the stairs. And Tony would tell me things he found out, too. We found comfort in conspiracy. The fear Mom and Dad always tried to hide frightened us.

It seems like a dream now. These days Mom lets me have slumber parties and lets me sleep over at other kids' houses. Tony was allowed to have a paper route. (He abandoned it after two months.) We could finally participate in school activities. See, Mom used to keep a tighter eye on us than suspicious old Mr. Humphrey, the sales clerk at the Seven Eleven.

We would have never been allowed to stay after school for any reason . . . even to learn the story behind a mysterious missing shepherd boy.

Chapter Seven

■

So much for my noble declaration on the playground. It really did look like we'd die trying to find that carving.

After two weeks of asking questions around school about a guy with an earring and sunglasses (a description fitting half the guys at school), we came up with nothing—zero, zilch, *nada*. Tony called Information for the number to the Israeli Embassy. He asked to talk to the woman investigating the Ten Brink/Yad Vashem case. She politely told him to bug off.

Mr. Ten Brink acted as if nothing had happened. Just a usual cold nod in the hallway. I knew the whole thing had hit rock bottom when Tony threw in the towel.

I was sitting on the porch trying to read *The Lion, the Witch, and The Wardrobe*. It's one of my favorite books. I've read it at least three times. But today I couldn't concentrate for beans. I didn't get much further than Lucy feeling the branches instead of the coats. Tony was cleaning parts of his motorcycle at the foot of the porch steps.

I sighed in exasperation and tossed the book down.

"There must be *something* else we can do," I muttered. Tony didn't answer.

"Maybe we could write to Yad Vashem. We could tell them the whole story and hopefully someone will—"

"Will you shut up about that stupid carving?" Tony suddenly snapped. He glared at me through his sandy brown bangs that had fallen down over his eyes. He tossed his head to flip them back and gave me one more look before he turned back to his carburetor.

"Fine," I scorned, "go ahead and give in. I refuse. I'm going to see Mr. Ten Brink on Monday and pump him for—"

"Leave Mr. Ten Brink alone!" Tony snarled. He jumped to his feet and took the four porch steps in one big leap. He stood over me, fists clenched, breathing hard. I blinked and stared at him in disbelief. Never in all my born days had I seen him so infuriated. Not even the day when he ran off to find Willie Watts after I had come home with a Willie-bloodied nose.

After a scalding glare, Tony threw down his cleaning rag and jerked the screen door open. He let it bang shut behind him.

I stared dismally at the chipped polish on my fingernails. (A futile attempt by Jackie to fashionize me.) I could understand how Tony felt. I didn't blame him, really.

I sighed. Tomorrow was Saturday. The past two Saturdays had been spent canvassing the high school neighborhood asking questions about Mr. Hairy Knuckles. Jackie had asked me to go shopping with her in Selby tomorrow. I didn't want to. I hate to shop for clothes. Books, yes. At least there was a Boersma Bookstore in the mall. Maybe I could pick up the latest Starr Cassidy adventure novel if it was out yet.

I dug into my jeans pocket to check my funds. Four crumpled dollar bills and a five. Barely enough for the book and McDonald's. And watermelon-flavored popcorn from The Poppe Shoppe. I winced. Time to accept another baby-sitting job, an activity just one notch below clothes shopping.

A day at the mall would probably be good for me, I mused as I stepped down the porch stairs and dropped onto the grass. I laid back spread-eagle, stared up at the blue sky, and wondered where the carving was this very instant. Perhaps on a pawnshop shelf, in between a guitar and a VCR.

Or maybe far away in an Arabic marketplace where a tur-baned man with yellow teeth and a scraggly beard hawked his wares. "See dis carving?" he'd shout at passersby. "Beddy, beddy baluable. Worth mega shekels." (Or whatever Arabic money is. Rubles? Wampum?) "Carved by Jewish boy in World War II."

Or maybe it was trading hands from Hairy Knuckles to a Japanese guy as an addition to his wooden shepherd collection "This is for your collection, Mr. Sushi," Hairy would say in a raspy voice. "That'll be a million bucks. I do take traveler's checks."

I hate to give up on anything. I pulled up a handful of grass and sprinkled it on my stomach. I hate even more to see Tony give up. I could only hope the carving was in safe hands somewhere until we could find it. Hope it wasn't being used as kindling wood this very moment by some skinhead, neo-Nazi fruitcake.

■ ■ ■

I shoveled in the last few bites of my Fruit Loops while Jackie stood in front of the dining room wall mirror and examined a new zit.

"Will you stop that?" I garbled over my Loops. "You're mak-ing me sick."

She dotted a blotch of cover-up on the offense and turned to me. "Is it noticeable?"

I looked at the whitish blob of makeup on Jackie's tanned face. "Not a bit," I replied. Friends are friends, after all. (Well it *wouldn't* be noticeable if you blinked your eyes really fast and shook your head while you looked at it.)

"Come on, the bus'll be here in five minutes," Jackie said.

I lifted the bowl to my lips and drank down the milk as I headed for the sink.

■ ■ ■

It's fun to ride the bus from Hamilton to Selby. The twenty-minute ride ends up being over an hour with the frequent stops and roundabout route. But it's interesting to see all the different people who take the bus.

It's the Saturday bus driver, however, who won me over to public transportation. One day about a year ago I stepped onto the bus and fumbled for my fare. I was just about to stick my quarters in when I accidentally stumbled, and my quarters clattered to the floor.

"Nice play, Shakespeare," the driver announced cheerfully.

I surfaced from retrieving my fare with a grin. I looked at the wise-guy bus driver, whose embroidered name patch on his shirt said "Gus." He was an older guy with a few gray streaks in his dark, wavy hair. His teeth were a little crooked, but I thought they looked cool. He grinned at me.

I gestured at his name patch. "*Gus*?" I snorted. "Yeah, right. Gus the bus driver."

The driver shoved his hat further up on his head and leaned back with a hand on his hip. "A rose by any other name would smell as sweet," he said in a mock growl. "So what's *your* name? Hildegarde?"

"No. It's Svetlana. *Miss* Svetlana to you," I replied as I dropped into a seat.

"Whatever you say, Winifred."

■ ■ ■

Now Jackie and I climbed aboard the bus, and Gus grinned at me as I popped my quarters into the slot.

"Good morning, Agnes. Haven't seen you in a while."

"How's it going, Frodo?"

Jackie and I headed for the back of the bus and sat down in front of an old lady. We deliberately didn't sit behind her. I mean, if I were old, I wouldn't want two young kids to sit behind me and have to wonder what they were up to.

We settled in and tucked our knees against the seats in front of us. Jackie ticked off on her fingers the things she had to purchase.

"I need to get a new pair of socks, a couple new pairs of panties . . ."

Panties! Another hated word!

"Underwear," I automatically corrected.

". . . a roll of film for my dad, a new curling iron if it's not too expensive—"

"There's a K-Mart near the mall if we have time."

"I think they may be on sale at Penney's. Uh, what else do I have to get . . . ?"

I watched the new arrivals from the last stop find their seats. A sweet-looking old black lady, wearing cat-eye glasses and carrying a little cage with a dog in it, sat down near Gus. Apparently she and the driver knew each other well, and they chatted away. A guy in a green army jacket with a sullen expression slouched down into a seat in front of us.

I thought back to the first time Jackie and I took the bus to Selby. We barely knew each other. It was just a few weeks after The Incident with Katie Wentworth. That hour-long bus ride was all it took to get down each other's life stories. Then we spent the day together like old friends.

I learned that day that Jackie was an only child and that

her dad wasn't her real dad. She'd never met her real father and said she didn't want to. He walked out on her and her mother when Jackie was only two. Until she was seven, it was just Jackie and her mother. Then her mom met a guy at the bank she worked at, and they got married.

I asked Jackie if it was hard to have a dad all of a sudden. It wasn't, she told me. Her mom was happy and even worked part-time now. She saw her mom more than ever. And Chris, her new dad (but she called him Dad, not Chris), was a really cool guy. He plays guitar in a Christian rock band called Jericho.

The D'Amicos moved to Hamilton from Selby last year. Chris wanted to get Jackie out of the big city and wanted more peace and quiet. Which is funny considering that he rehearses in their basement with a screaming, screeching electric guitar. It's also funny that he's a lawyer. A longhaired lawyer who plays in a Christian rock band. Even my mom laughed at that one.

Two more passengers got on the bus. A huge lady took up two side seats, and a creepy guy sat down three seats up and on the other side from us. I was glad he didn't sit any closer.

"Oh!" Jackie suddenly gasped. "Don't let me forget to get a birthday present for my mom! It's tomorrow."

"Birthday present, birthday present," I murmured with my eyes closed as I pressed my fingertips on my temples. I said the words six more times, pressing my temples each time. A sure-fire way to make yourself remember something.

"I have no idea what to get her," Jackie groaned. My gaze wandered over to the creepy guy. I like to keep tabs on potential situations.

"Perfume? Nah. The last bottle I got her isn't even half gone."

He was your typical avoidable. A mean-looking bully with dark sunglasses and his black hair slicked back into a ponytail.

"Stationery?" Jackie wondered. "Nah. She has a drawer full of stationery."

He had gold chains around his neck.

"Maybe a microwave popcorn popper. But I'd probably use it more than she would."

And a diamond-crusted ruby in one ear. I sat straight up. Mr. Ten Brink's description of the guy he'd given the statue to . . .

"What about one of those Chia pets? She likes plants."

His hands were shoved in his pockets. Come on, buddy, just show me your hands. Do something. Scratch your head, rub your chin. My nose began to tingle.

"Maybe some bubble bath junk. I don't know." I barely heard her.

The guy glanced outside, waited a few seconds, then pulled a hand out of his pocket to reach up and hit the buzzer.

The knuckles were hairy.

The bus rumbled to a halt, and I grabbed Jackie's arm and dragged her to the back door. The creep lit a cigarette as he headed for the front door.

"Are you crazy?" Jackie demanded. "Our stop is not for five minutes yet!"

"See ya, Francis!" Gus called out.

"Uh, yeah yeah yeah. See ya, Henry."

The doors opened, and I hauled a protesting Jackie down the steps and onto the curb.

"Come on!" I yelled and turned to follow the guy.

"Not until you tell me what's going on this instant!"

I ran the few steps back to Jackie.

"Hairy Knuckles!" I hissed excitedly. "The guy on the bus was Hairy Knuckles!"

Chapter Eight

■

W<small>HAT!"</small> J<small>ACKIE</small> <small>SHOUTED IN MY EAR.</small>

I had no time to stand around and have a tea party. I grabbed her arm and propelled her down the sidewalk.

"He was on the bus, I'm telling you. Medium build, dark hair slicked back in a ponytail, and a ruby earring circled with diamonds—just like Mr. Ten Brink said, remember? Hurry!"

"What do you intend to do once we catch up with him?" Jackie panted as she struggled to keep pace with me. "Ask him to hand over the carving like a good little villain?"

She irritated me. Partly because I hadn't thought that far ahead. Only Starr Cassidy could whip out her school ID, confront a hulking menace, and make a citizen's arrest. It didn't work like that outside of novels. But we were wasting time.

"I don't know. We'll make it up as we go—follow our gut."

"Oh, great."

"Come on!"

We wove in and out of people as I struggled to keep Hairy Knuckles in sight. I bumped into a woman ushering two little kids down the sidewalk. She glared at me. "Sorry," I mumbled. I looked at the spot where I'd last seen Hairy. He'd vanished!

I ran faster, then stopped, panicky and frustrated. Where

could he have gone so fast? I looked ahead and across the street, then spotted him as he pulled open the door to a candy store just past the Selby Public Museum.

"There!" I shouted. "He just went into Millie's Candy Store. Come on!"

I started to run, but Jackie yanked me back.

"Casey, we can't just burst in there like a SWAT team. We have to have a plan."

I frowned and thought. Then I snapped my fingers.

"Your mom's birthday present! You could get her a box of candy. We'll just go in as casual as anything, and while you shop for candy, I'll look around and case the joint."

"You'll what?"

"Come on!"

We crossed the street, walked past the museum, and approached the store. I swallowed hard as I pulled the door open.

The store was dimly lit, not bright and cheery like you'd expect a candy store to be. It smelled sickeningly sweet. A seedy-looking kid a few years older than me stood behind the counter, twirling a paper cone around in a cotton candy machine. We walked over to the glass case and stared at the rows of chocolates and confections.

The kid looked up and coughed a smoker's cough. He drew a sleeve across his nose.

"What do ya need?" he asked in an anything but friendly voice.

I nudged Jackie. "Uh, do you have any boxed candy?" she asked in a higher tone than usual. "It's for a present."

The kid gestured at a wall behind us and turned back to the cotton candy. For the first time I sent a complete glance around the small store. No Hairy Knuckles! But we didn't see him leave!

We walked over to the shelves and pretended to busily inspect the boxes. Most of it looked as if it'd been on the shelf a long time. We peered at grayish pieces of chocolate through dusty cellophane. Jackie wrinkled her nose and threw me a look. I turned back to the clerk.

"Do you have a bathroom?"

"Yeah."

"Is it occupied?"

Was it my imagination or did the kid's eyes narrow a bit?

"No. Why?"

"I have to use it."

"Employees only."

"Oh," I replied. *Nice guy*, I thought. *A real charmer.*

I turned back to Jackie, who poked at the boxes in contempt.

"I wouldn't give this to a starving child," she whispered disgustedly. "Let's get out of here. I'm scared, and I want to go to the mall."

I didn't buy the scared bit from Katie Wentworth's master.

"Look," I whispered back, "you wait here. I'm going to the bathroom so I can see if there's a back exit or whatever."

"You can't. Didn't you just hear the slimeball over there?"

"Watch me."

Some kids turn their eyelids inside out. Some kids burp the alphabet. I can fake throw-up with the best of them. It's a genuine talent. Once when my mom was in the living room, I stood in the kitchen with a cup full of water and apple chunks. I stood there making the most marvelous noises—heaving, retching, and generally dying. After a terrific roar I threw the contents of the cup to the floor in a splat. My mom made a beeline for the bathroom with her hand over her mouth.

So when I gave a weak cough, then a stronger one, Jackie rolled her eyes. She knew what was coming.

I coughed harder and put a hand to my forehead, then looked at my palm and wiped it on my jeans like it was full of sweat. I turned and started back to the counter, swaying a bit. I reached the counter and leaned against it heavily. I coughed again and started to pant.

"I think it's the smell in here," I groaned. "I think I'm gonna get sick."

The kid's lip curled. "Get sick somewhere else."

I doubled over as a heave racked my body. A superb, guttural retching that sounded like it was about to bring up a whole Thanksgiving dinner rose from my throat. It was the performance of my life, and I gloried in it. For effect, I let some spit dribble out—a promise of things to come—then clapped my hand over my mouth and stared wide-eyed at the kid.

He stared wide-eyed back. He jumped to open a door at his left and jerked his thumb down the hallway. With one hand over my mouth and one clutching my stomach, I shuffled hunchbacked past him.

He shut the door on my misery. I gave a few more loud heaving noises over my shoulder as I continued down the hallway, past the bathroom. I reached the end and found a staircase that led up to a door.

Oh boy.

A reality check made me hesitate. What on earth was I doing? About to prance up some stairs that led to a room with Hairy Knuckles in it? It was probably his apartment. The apartment of a loser who stole stuff from old people—a guy without any conscience. I closed my eyes and conjured up a picture of Mr. Ten Brink the Wronged. Duty made me draw a deep breath and place my foot on the first step.

I pulled myself up and placed my foot on step number two. I was nuts, crazy, over the edge. I should have listened to Tony.

Step three, four, five. My heart slammed against my rib cage. I half hoped Jackie would come storming down the hallway to drag me out of there. (Protesting, naturally.)

I closed my eyes again and imagined Hans. His one living desire was to see the Ten Brink family honored at Yad Vashem. I clenched my teeth. Step six, seven.

I was halfway up when I thought I heard voices. At least two, but I couldn't tell.

Step eight, nine, ten, eleven. I found myself at the top of the stairs, only a few feet from the door. My nose tingled as I inched closer to it. I could definitely hear the voices now, but they were low and indistinct. As I shifted my weight to bend closer to hear, a floor board creaked beneath my feet.

The voices stopped.

The door flew open! And there, filling the doorway with his not so medium-build bulk, stood Hairy Knuckles. I stared up at him, petrified as stone.

He wore an Elvis Presley sneer that revealed a row of even, white teeth. I noticed them because I'm a teeth person. Probably because I happen to have a set of rather nice teeth, and I've never had braces. (It's one of my few redeeming features; sue me for my pride.)

His dark hair shone. The ropes of gold gleamed. The ruby/diamond earring sparkled. His sunglasses were stuck in his front shirt pocket by an earpiece, so I could see his light brown eyes. And I saw something odd there.

Something . . . something strange that didn't seem to fit his tough-guy appearance.

At least for a minute.

"Who is it?" a gravelly voice said behind him.

Suddenly the eyes hardened into bits of cold stone. I turned and made to bolt for the stairs. A hand clamped down on my shoulder. I opened my mouth to scream, but the other hand clapped it off in a pipsqueak yelp.

He yanked me to himself, dragged me inside, and kicked the door shut.

Chapter
Nine

∎

HE SHOVED ME INTO A WORN, GREEN, UPHOLSTERED CHAIR where I cowered and trembled and fought to keep down my Fruit Loops.

Well, I'd found Hairy Knuckles at last. Had him right where I wanted him. Just flash him the school ID and I'd be on my way with the carving.

Color me stupid.

The other voice belonged to a guy who stood by a dirty window. He seemed to be about Hairy's age or so, mid-thirties I guessed—and even more villainous looking. At least Hairy had the appearance of a classic hoodlum; this gorilla looked like the type other hoodlums avoided.

"Personified evil" is a good start at describing him. He stood with his arms held tensely at his sides, like he was about to snatch a six-shooter from an invisible holster and gun down Wyatt Earp at the OK Corral. He stared at me with a glower, eyes inky black with a maniacal glint. His thick, black hair was brushed back from his forehead and fell to his shoulders in greasy, curly waves. A patchy beard filled his face. Patchy because a scar curved through it from one ear down to his chin. I wondered how many stitches it took to close a wound like that.

"Who is she?" Gorilla said hoarsely and with an accent.

His lips barely moved when he talked. His eyes bored laser beams into me, and I was sure I would faint. I'd never done such a sissy thing, but so help me, I wouldn't have minded at that moment.

"Who are you?" Hairy asked.

I turned my attention back to him. I could talk to him. The other guy paralyzed my tongue.

"Ju—just a kid." My chin shook like it was 10 below zero in the room.

"I can see that."

"I—I'm just h-h-here for the c-c-carving."

"The what?" Gorilla said with a voice that sounded like metal scrapings. I didn't look at him. I concentrated on Hairy. A nice, normal scumbag.

"The c-c-carving you took from Mr. Ten Brink."

"How does she know about that?" Gorilla asked.

"Yeah," Hairy said as he gave my chair a shove. "How *do* you know about that?"

Hello, 9-1-1? I thought to myself bleakly. *Got a situation here . . .*

"Who do you work for, kid?" Gorilla asked as he moved away from the window and slowly came my way. My pulse-rate jumped to heart attack proportions. His heavy boots clumped ominously on the wooden floor. His black eyes promised danger. His lips curved in what I took to be a smile. A hideous smile.

I wanted my mommy.

"Eh, she don't work for no one," Hairy said. "I remember now. I saw her in the hallway when I went to get the carving."

Gorilla stopped. He looked at me with obvious regret and turned away. He sat down on the dirty green couch near the window and propped his feet on the coffee table. I stared at his boots. Steel-toed, black leather motorcycle boots. I saw a slit on the ankle side of one boot with a knife tucked in it.

"Sloppy work, friend. That isn't like you."

Hairy shrugged as he cleaned out the crud from under his fingernails. "We all have our days."

Gorilla slid the knife out of his boot, then traced his finger along the blade.

"So, kid, what did you hear at the door?"

"Noth—" my voice squeaked. I tried again. "Nothing."

I watched, mesmerized, as the finger he ran along the blade left a trail of crimson on the shining metal. Raw fear coated my stomach like Pepto-Bismol. At least I knew what it felt like *before* one fainted. Dizzy, oxygen-starved, little black dots sparkling around me . . .

"Aw, you're scaring the little ankle-biter," Hairy drawled as he planted a boot on the arm of my chair and shined a dull spot on his cowboy boot with a hankie. "She's a nothing. We're wasting time."

"What do you want the carving for?" Gorilla grated, still toying with the knife.

"It belongs to Mr. Ten Brink," I heard myself say in a far-off voice. "His family . . . the Avenue of the Righteous . . ."

"The carving will soon be in a place you will only read about, my little worthless friend."

"Caseeeyyy!" I heard a voice shout from the bottom of the stairs.

Hairy and Gorilla exchanged swift glances. Jackie's yell made me blink. I shook my head and sucked in air.

"That's my friend. Just give me the carving and—" My bravado melted at the look on Gorilla's cold-blooded face.

"Outta my way, you worm!" Jackie's shout floated up the stairs. "Casey!"

Gorilla nodded at Hairy, who grabbed my shirt behind my neck and lifted me out of my seat. He threw me roughly toward the door. I lost my balance and fell forward, skidding on the floor on my face. I was so scared, I barely felt the impact. Hairy grabbed my arm and pulled me up, less harshly this time, and hustled me to the door. He jerked it open, walked out with me, and shut the door behind him. He turned me to the side and shoved me against the wall with both arms. His fingers dug into my shoulders.

"Listen to me and listen good," he whispered in a different tone—not the arrogant drawl I'd heard in the room. He brought his head down nose-to-nose with mine. I stared, not blinking, not breathing, into those fierce amber eyes.

"Forget this place. Forget the carving. You come back again and I let him kill you. Clear?"

I nodded and hoped he could tell the difference between my nod and my shaking. He shoved me toward the stairs.

"Get outta here, buzzard bait!" he said loudly in the former drawl, then laughed as he went back into the room and slammed the door.

Somehow my legs walked me to the stairway. They nearly gave way a few times on the descent though. I dragged my hands along the walls for support. Jackie waited at the bottom of the steps with the kid creep, who now looked like St. Peter to me. Jackie gasped at my face, and I wondered for the first time what kissing the floor had done to me.

"Are you all right?"

"Let's just get out of here."

■ ■ ■

I sank into the last-row seat of the bus and buried my face in my arms. Mercifully, Jackie didn't demand an explanation. She placed a protective arm around my shoulders.

I practiced breathing slowly and deeply, savoring life.

"We have to find Tony and Marty right away when we get home," I whispered eventually.

"Sure, we will," Jackie answered soothingly.

"I mean it, Jackie. We can't waste any time."

"Your lip is bleeding. I think I have a Kleenex in my purse." She searched her handbag and pressed the tissue into my hand.

I dabbed my lower lip and looked at the stained tissue. It reminded me of the blood on Gorilla's knife, and my stomach flip-flopped. But I wasn't going to throw up now. And I had to stop this wimpy shaking. I shook off Jackie's arm and composed myself while I told her in a flat monotone exactly what had happened.

All the color drained from Jackie's face. Now *she* trembled. I wondered if I had looked as white as she did now when I sat in that chair.

I ran my tongue over my lower lip. It had started to swell. The scrape on my chin stung a bit. I had a funny feeling, though, that Hairy Knuckles hadn't meant for me to fall.

■ ■ ■

We found Tony in the garage, checking the oil under the hood of Mom's mini-van. He was cleaning the dipstick with a rag when he saw us and froze. He looked at my lip, then into my eyes.

He came over to me and lifted my chin as he surveyed the damage.

For the first time, my eyes filled with tears.

"W-we have to c-call Marty," I finally managed. I turned away from Tony, furious with myself. I remain dry-eyed as I face two sleazy reprobates who could easily become the instruments of my demise, yet blubber like a baby at the first flicker of sympathy from my brother. Pathetic on a stick, that's me.

Jackie ducked into the house to phone Marty. Tony turned back to quickly finish his business with the van. Jackie reappeared and told us Marty was on his way.

■ ■ ■

And so the four of us sat over Cokes at the table in the pool house.

The pool house is my favorite place. It's an annex from the garage and adjacent to our built-in swimming pool. It's one large, comfy room with a fireplace at one end and a kitchen of sorts at the other. Cushioned benches line the walls. It's a great place to entertain—slumber parties, youth group get-togethers from Hamilton Bible Church, Mom and Dad's New Year's Eve parties.

It's also great for privacy. My favorite place to read. So we had no fear of anyone overhearing our conversation.

I started at the beginning, when I first spotted Hairy Knuckles on the bus. I told them the whole story but left out a few details. Like the nearly fainting part. And the part about Hairy's eyes. How he seemed to know me.

I finished, and everyone sat in silence.

Marty turned to Jackie. "Are you all right?"

My sore jaw dropped as low as pain tolerance allowed. I didn't see any facial blemishes on *Jackie* (other than the zit). I didn't hear *Jackie* spew out an incredible, life-threatening tale. The concern in Marty's eyes made me want to throw my Coke in his face.

"Yeah, are you okay?" Tony asked her too.

Make that two Cokes. I stared up beyond the ceiling and pled for sanity in a world gone wrong.

Marty sat back in his chair and looked at me, shaking his head in a dazed manner. "I can't believe you went up those stairs."

Well, finally. I shrugged self-consciously. "Well, I had to find—"

Marty continued, "Of all the lunatic, idiotic—"

Tony broke in. "—stupid, irresponsible—"

"Hey!" Jackie interrupted angrily. "Can't you see what she's been through? She's the bravest person I've ever met. No way would I have gone up those stairs. But she did—for Mr. Ten Brink . . . and for Hans."

Maybe Jackie was my *first* best friend. I assumed an injured air and swirled the ice around in my glass.

Tony stood up and began to pace. "No, it's not bravery. You could have gotten killed, Casey! These guys are way out of your league! Casey, this is not one of your adventure stories, all right? Look at your lip! It could have been a lot worse!" He plunked down onto a bench in frustration and rubbed his face with his hands.

I figured he wouldn't believe me if I told him I didn't think Hairy meant to do it. I wasn't sure *I* believed it yet.

But there was something else. Something I didn't tell even Jackie. It had to wait until we were all together.

"I saw the carving."

Tony's head snapped up. Marty choked on a swallow from his glass, and pop dribbled out of his nose as he sputtered and reached for a napkin.

"You *saw* it?" Jackie whispered in awe. Tony got up and sat at the table.

I remembered the steel-toed motorcycle boots and a slit with a knife tucked inside, and I shuddered.

"When Gorilla put his feet on the table," I said softly as I stared at a spot on the tablecloth. "It was a glass tabletop. I could see through, just in front of the boots, to the bottom shelf of the table. There was a small bundle. Something wrapped in old, cracked brown leather."

I squeezed my eyes shut and stifled a groan. I had been in the same room with it! I could have reached over and touched it, I was so close.

"There's nothing you could have done," Marty said firmly.

"Mr. Gorilla would have had you for lunch," Tony agreed.

I sighed. "At least we know where it is."

"What's that supposed to mean?" Tony challenged.

I looked at him sideways. "What do you think it means?"

I braced myself for his reaction. I wrapped my legs around the legs of my chair and waited for the monsoon to hit. Waited for him to tell me a very hot place would freeze over before we'd go back to rescue the carving.

Instead, he pinched his upper lip and thought. I let him think while I debated on telling everyone the other odd fact I had held back.

Hairy had lied to Gorilla. He said he had seen me in the hallway the day he took the carving. He did that to save my skin, but why? He had no conscience. At least, not in the stealing arena. Maybe creeps have certain codes. Do this, but never that. Make old men miserable, reduce the population with drive-by shootings, sell drugs to first-graders, but hey—draw the line at smacking a kid. My brain refused to accept any other notion. In a distant corner of my mind I knew Gorilla could have ignored Hairy and killed me. But I didn't want to think about that.

I pondered Hairy's hoodlum hypocrisy. At least Gorilla looked like a dedicated little villain.

"What's the matter, Jackie?" Marty asked.

Jackie stared at the air with intense concentration. Then she banged her hands on the table. My glass jumped.

"Alex Wendell!" she shouted triumphantly. "The scumbag!"

"You mean the kid behind the counter? You *know* him?"

She nodded. "He was a few grades ahead of me at Hiawatha. I knew he seemed familiar, but I couldn't figure out from where."

"Wow," I whispered. "This could prove very interesting."

Tony grinned and looked at Marty. "Maybe we could pay Alex a visit."

I snorted. "Even *I* could handle him."

We all sat with scheming expressions on our faces. I myself pictured this Alex sitting at a table and squinting under a bright light, cowering under a ruthless interrogation.

"Awright, you degenerate," I'd say with a Brooklyn accent, "if youse knows what is good for youse, youse betta high-tail your sorry self up them stairs at Millie's and don't come down till youse gots the carving."

Marty interrupted my private visions.

"Hey, guys," he said with a shrug and a funny expression on his face. The same expression when he once told me I was his best friend.

"It's obvious we have something going here, with the four of us. Know what I mean?"

"No, I don't," Tony said.

"*I'm* confused," I quipped.

"Well, you know," he said exasperatedly, "a club-type thing. Like a gang or an association. Like a we're-all-in-this-thing-together thing, okay? Do I have to spell it out?"

"It would help," Jackie suggested.

"I think I know what you mean," I answered. "We're all in this together to help Mr. Ten Brink. It almost seems like we need a name for ourselves."

Tony rolled his eyes. "You mean like we're a detective agency or something. I think I'm gonna be sick."

"No, not like a detective agency," Marty explained. "Like a . . . *helper* agency."

"But Mr. Ten Brink doesn't even *want* our help. He doesn't even know what we're doing," Jackie pointed out.

"Maybe that'll be one of the characteristics of our . . . society. We help people *secretly*," Marty said.

We mulled on this. I liked the idea. It reminded me of the verse Pastor Mullins had talked about in church the previous week. About when you give, you shouldn't let your right hand know what your left hand is doing.

"Yeah, a secret helper agency," I said as I stared up at the ceiling. I liked the sound of it.

"What would we call ourselves?" Tony asked doubtfully. I was amazed he even considered the idea.

What *would* we call ourselves? I thought about this, and something started to tumble around in my brain. Bits and pieces of this whole adventure—a *secretly* hidden Jewish boy, a carving stolen for a *hidden* reason—seemed to suggest a certain name.

Besides, it's what started it all in the first place.

"I've got it," I announced. They all looked at me, and I looked back at them. Marty the Redhaired, Jackie the Beautiful, Tony the Often Annoying. Four of us, at the start of something quite possibly wonderful.

"We'll call ourselves . . . the Classifieds."

Chapter Ten

■

I SIDETRACK EASILY. NOW ALL I WANTED TO DO WAS ESTABLISH THE ground rules for our new club—the Classifieds.

We'd help people who didn't necessarily ask for our help. People who didn't necessarily deserve it. We'd make people believe once again in peace, love, and brotherhood. Or something like that.

I got up, went to a drawer, and rummaged for some paper and a pen.

"What are you doing?" Tony asked.

"I'm going to draw up the charter for our new club."

"We don't have time for that," Jackie said. "We have to come up with a plan to get the carving back."

"Didn't you say that Gorilla said it would be in a faraway place very soon?" Marty asked.

I sighed and gave up my search.

"What do you know about this Alex guy?" Tony asked Jackie as I plopped back into my seat.

"Not very much," she admitted. "He hung out with a bad crowd—"

"That's obvious," I interjected.

"—but seemed like a quiet guy. Not really the bully type."

"Do you know where he lives?"

"No. And there's probably a lot of Wendells in the phone book."

"Well, there's only one thing to do then," Tony said thoughtfully. "Anyone else have a sweet tooth?"

■ ■ ■

The stores in Selby don't close until 9, so we had a little time to do some planning. Mom and Dad were going out with Marty's parents, so Dad said it was okay for Tony to use the van tonight.

We told Mom and Dad that the four of us planned to grab a bite to eat together, then *maybe* catch a movie. Absolutely true. We simply left out the part about cornering a junior hood and third-degreeing him into cooperation.

Jackie went home to change, and Mom and I shared the bathroom mirror as we readied ourselves for our very different evenings.

Tony had suggested that I wear makeup or something to help disguise myself, so Alex wouldn't recognize me immediately and create a scene. I had already tracked down a beach hat and sunglasses and had changed my clothing. The makeup would be the tough part.

I poked unhappily at my mom's variety of makeup as she swept mascara onto her eyelashes. Lipstick. Eyeliner. Cover Girl Clean Makeup. I didn't see what was clean about it. Tiny boxes of colorful stuff that I took to be eyeshadow. Zit cover-up. Blush. Lipliner. I stared at the bewildering mess and wondered how my mother made sense of it all.

I observed her out of the corner of my eye as I picked up a tube and pretended to know exactly what to do with it. I liked the way she wore makeup—so it didn't look like it. But it always impressed me how she looked after she came out of the bathroom. Marty's mom, on the other hand, wore it like she was advertising for a play at the local civic theater. Vivid splotches of turquoise on her lids (always turquoise), two slashes of blush on her cheeks, and foundation about four shades darker than her natural color. You could always see the line just under her jaw where the makeup ended and her white neck began.

I frowned as I stared at myself in the mirror. Why didn't I wind up with Mom's eye color? Hers were sky-blue. Mine were a combination of Dad's brown eyes and Mom's blue—a weird hazel. My sandy-brown hair hung in a nondescript style to my shoulders. Mom's blonde hair *flowed.* I parted my lips to look at my teeth and feel better about myself. At least I inherited Mom's smile.

Mom had already questioned me about the swollen lip and the scrape on my chin. I had answered truthfully that I fell, which came as no surprise to her. She simply sighed and told me to be more careful.

I hurried to get some of the makeup on.

"That's lipliner, Casey," Mom said gently. "It doesn't go on your eyes."

Crud. I stared ruefully at the tube and tossed it on the pile.

"Have a seat," Mom said as she gestured at the toilet. I closed the lid and sat down. Mom studied me a minute, then selected a few items from the pile and went to work.

She was probably shocked that I subjected myself to this facial, so she didn't make a big deal out of it. Wise mother. I did see a smile almost sneak past the corner of her mouth. This was a mother/daughter thing, this makeup business, and I knew how ridiculously happy something like this made her.

Mom didn't plan on having a tomboy for a daughter. I spent the first five years of my life in adorable dresses and cute hairdos. After that, I orchestrated a mutiny. I stashed all my dresses and frilly hair accessories in a bag and at the age of six marched down to the Salvation Army and stuffed it in the donation box. (Tony told me I was going to get it, and I got it. But Mom got the point and realized she wouldn't have a prancing sissy for a daughter. Barring any special occasions—I had to give a little too—I had spent the rest of my life in jeans.)

At this proximity, I could smell Mom's peppermint-gum breath and see the smile lines around her eyes. I didn't really mind all this fussing, to a point. It made Mom happy.

Mom stood back and surveyed me, then smiled. I swallowed. What did I look like? Mrs. Behrens? At least Mom didn't use any turquoise stuff.

My mother pointed at the mirror. "Take a look."

I held my breath and turned to my reflection.

"Hey," I said in surprise, "not bad."

My eyes didn't look so ho-hum. They looked *noticeable*, but not in the Mrs. Behrens kind of way. Mom did a great job of concealing the scrape on my chin, and even made my lip look less puffy. My cheeks had a subtle hint of color, unlike my usual pale complexion. And the zit that had threatened to rename me Nirvana of the Third Eye had vanished.

"You did a good job, Mom," I said approvingly but not too heartily. I didn't want her to think we'd make a habit of this.

Mom shrugged. "I had a great face to work with. Makeup only enhances beauty."

Moms are supposed to say that stuff, but I smiled anyway. I threw my arms around her and hugged her, happy she was my mom. She hugged me tightly back.

■ ■ ■

Though I knew they were all waiting for me, as I walked out of the bathroom and into the living room an enormous sense of self-consciousness crashed down on me. Now I knew why I didn't wear makeup.

Marty broke off in mid-sentence to stare at me. Tony followed his gaze and did the same. Jackie beamed. Dad poked his head around the corner from the kitchen (probably in response to Mom's prompting) and gave a whistle.

I wanted to crawl into a hole.

I gave them a vicious glare that dared even one of them to make a comment.

"Well, what do you say we get going, eh?" Marty jumped up and headed for the door. The others followed, and I scurried along behind them, my face flaming.

"Have a good time," Dad called after us. "Drive carefully, Tony, and park it away from other cars, okay?"

Dad has a door ding thing. Tony yelled back his agreement. Since I was the last one out, I heard what Mom said to Dad.

"When was the last time Casey and Tony went out together?"

"No idea."

"Well, it's nice to see them having fun together."

I thought about where we were going, and the word *fun* did not come racing into my mind. We were about to confront a criminal-in-training. And what guarantee did we have that we wouldn't run into my two favorite creeps? I put on my neon green sunglasses and hoped my disguise worked.

Fun? Ha.

■ ■ ■

I stared out the window on the way to Selby and wondered what a carob tree looked like.

I hoped it blossomed with big, fragrant flowers. White. I could imagine a whole grove of them, row after row, with the wind gently waving the leaves and flowers, so you could smell the beautiful fragrance when you sat beneath them. And you'd stare at those trees and wonder about all of them and wish you knew the story behind each one. But the trees would stand silent, keeping to themselves the wonderful reasons they were planted.

If I could sit beneath a tree in the grove called the Avenue of the Righteous, I would close my eyes and picture the faces of the rescued Jewish people. I'd imagine massive crowds, like a hundred overflowing Rose Bowl stadiums—a cheering, living affront to Hitler's plan of devastation. And I would be glad for the heroes of the persecuted.

I remembered the medallion Mr. Ten Brink had told me about, given to each person who planted a tree there. On one side of the medallion is an engraving of a thin arm stretching up through barbed wire to a globe, a world it cannot reach. On the other side is a likeness of Yad Vashem and an inscription from something called *The Mishnah*: "He who saves one life, it is as if he saves the whole world."

I shook my head in wonder at the magnificent idea somebody had of planting trees to honor those who had protected the victims of evil tyranny. Something to endure for generations, just like the generations the heroes had saved. I wished Hans could have walked through the Avenue of the Righteous and pointed out to his grandchildren the tree of the ones who saved him—who saved *them*.

"See there, little Willem?" Hans would have said in an old man's voice. "This tree was planted for my best friend, Johann. And for Johann's mama and papa. And for a man named Gerrit who found me on a train, and for a woman named Rene who fed me."

"Why did you wait so long, Hans?" I whispered. I added

that to the list of questions I'll ask when I get to heaven. Along with why are people born with an appendix. (I'd had mine taken out and saw no good reason to have it in the first place.)

One thing was certain. For whatever reason Hairy and Gorilla wanted the carving, it would never be as important as a new carob tree at Yad Vashem.

"McDonald's or Burger King?" Tony interrupted my Dream State.

We pulled into a drive-thru and ate in the car as we continued on to Selby. I watched as Jackie tore the end off a ketchup packet, then one by one dipped her fries into it. Painfully neat. I squirted a few packets all over, made sure Jackie saw the mess first, then commenced eating.

"What if Alex isn't working tonight?" Marty mumbled over his Big Mac.

"He has to be," I answered. Marty could be just like Jackie sometimes. He has the nasty habit of being practical when the occasion doesn't call for it.

Jackie handed me her compact and a lipstick. "Here. You ate off your lipstick."

"I didn't eat it off. I took it off before I ate. I didn't want my dinner to taste like Revlon."

"Go easy, it's a dark color."

I went to work and presented myself to Jackie for approval. She grimaced and removed a smudge below my lower lip with her finger. Then she nodded.

"You look great."

"Thanks," I mumbled as I readjusted my hat.

As we pulled onto Franklin Avenue, a few butterflies—or french fries—did a little dance in my stomach. Tony parked in the lot behind the museum, a decent distance from possible door dingers.

Tony turned around in the seat and laid it all out.

"Okay, here's the deal. Marty and I go into the store first, straight to the counter. You girls follow behind and go to the shelves, or look out the window. Just don't face the counter. When we have his attention, we'll—"

"Holey sock-a-moley!" I shouted, pointing at the crosswalk.

There stood Alex Wendell, head down, hands shoved deep in his pockets, waiting for the pedestrian crossing light to turn white. His direction was opposite that of the candy store. He was leaving!

I just don't think sometimes.

In a flash I had the door open. "Hey!" I shouted as I waved my arms.

Alex looked around, saw me, and turned his attention back to the crossing light.

"Hey, Alex!"

He jerked his head back toward me, then saw the other three pile out of the van. He backed up a few steps, glancing wildly in all directions.

"Real subtle, Casey," Tony groaned.

"We just want to talk to you!" I ignored Tony and trotted toward Alex, who gave up waiting for the crossing light and stepped down onto the street. Traffic was too heavy though, and he couldn't make a dash across the road yet. The others followed my move, and the gap closed between the Classifieds and Alex the Soon-to-be-interrogated.

The light turned white, and Alex took off. The only thing I thought about as the four of us jogged after him was what an utter waste of my mom's good makeup this disguise had turned out to be.

Chapter Eleven

■

*I*T TOOK TWO CITY BLOCKS TO CATCH UP WITH HIM. HE RAN FAST but proved no match for the Most Valuable Player of the Year on the Beverly High football team. Tony grabbed him, held him by his shirt behind his neck, and waited for the rest of us to arrive.

My brother can be fairly diplomatic at times, so it didn't surprise me that he had Alex calmed and subdued by the time Jackie, Marty, and I puffed to a stop next to them.

"Hey," the junior hood yelled at me, "he said he's your brother. Tell him I had nothing to do with your fat lip!"

"He knows that, Alex. We just want to talk to you."

Tony relaxed his grip, and Alex leaned against the brick wall of the Selby Community Bank. We stood in a half-circle around him. He darted a glance at me and Jackie, then looked at the ground. His gaze stayed there while he spoke.

"Look, I ain't got no beef with you guys, okay?" he said in a low tone, breathing hard from the run. "It ain't me you got the problem with. And you probably won't believe me, but when I saw you come down the stairs looking like you did, I told myself that was it. I finished my shift and just left the store, but they don't know it's for good."

He looked into my eyes then, and my underdog mentality waved banners and hung out flags to let me know that despite this kid's seedy appearance, before me stood a genuine victim—the biggest underdog I'd ever personally known.

Beverly High is in a fairly upscale neighborhood—at least compared to Hiawatha High School. We have our share of fry-brains and no-goods, but not too many who look like Alex Wendell.

He had a cornered look in his light blue eyes. His hands trembled as he lit the cigarette he had pulled from a pack in his pocket. He wore the same dirty shirt I remembered from this morning (was it only this morning?). It was screen-printed on the front with a sickening logo from a heavy-metal band—a skeleton with worms coming out of its eyes and swastikas all over. He had the name of the band tattooed on the skinny bicep of one arm.

But his eyes struck me the most. Hunted, empty, tired, afraid. I could almost hear Pastor Mullins say something about the eyes being the windows of the soul.

Allowing a smidgen of compassion to show through (without shedding my tough-girl image—we still had to get some info out of this guy), I said, "We aren't going to hurt you, Alex. We just need a little information."

He snorted. The cigarette bounced up and down as he talked. "Yeah, right. Who doesn't need a little information. Why don't you just tell me who you work for? Who sent you to the store today? They're idiots if they thought Kahlil and Burns would give *you* anything." He broke into a scornful laugh. "You gotta lose the good-girl image if you wanna do business with them. You don't fool me."

I wanted to ask what was wrong with a good-girl image, but suddenly felt like I did the day I fell from climbing Mr. Sanchez's trellis and slammed the air out of my lungs.

"What did you say?" I asked breathlessly.

He looked at me uncertainly.

"The names of the guys upstairs," I said, feeling dizzy and weak all at once.

He shrugged and looked at me as though my upstairs bulb had burned out. "Ahmed Kahlil and Robbie Burns."

Robbie Burns. Robbie Burns. Robbie Burns.

I slowly turned my gaze to Tony. He stared back at me, his blue eyes shocked, disbelieving.

"What's going on?" Marty demanded as he looked from Tony to me.

"Yeah, what's going on?" Alex said nervously.

Tony shook his head the tiniest fraction at me. I gave him a tiny nod back.

"We gotta talk to you, my friend," Tony answered in a dangerous tone as his eyes bore in on Alex. "*Now*."

■ ■ ■

Alex seemed willing enough to talk, even if just from curiosity. He told us about a hotdog joint not far away where we could sit and not be bothered.

I watched him out of the corner of my eye as we walked together. Though he didn't say a word and the tough expression on his face didn't change, I sensed something that Tony would have called nonsense. I felt like he was almost glad to be with us, with people who looked normal.

I couldn't think about Alex long though, because all I saw in my mind were a pair of light brown eyes that should have belonged to a gangster but didn't. The mystery behind the carving had become all the more bewildering.

Hairy Knuckles was Robbie Burns. Undercover FBI agent. Christian. And thief.

■ ■ ■

The hotdog joint was just that . . . a greasy-spoon type of dive that, according to Alex, sold the city's best hotdogs. Well, I happen to be a connoisseur (now there's a word for you—my dad says it's someone who can tell the difference between something lame and something outstanding) of hotdogs. Despite the fact that I'd just consumed a cheeseburger and fries, I ordered a Chicago-style dog and silently dared the waitress to bring me something less than the genuine article.

To my surprise, they delivered. Right down to the cucumber slices and jalapeño peppers. (I must confess, I do not eat the jalapeños. But even the removal of them leaves a nice memory.)

The hotdog tasted great. I finished it off and wiped my mouth as I looked again at the menu stuck between the napkin holder and the salt and pepper shakers. Delbert's Dazzling Dogs. I'd have to remember this place.

We were sitting in a corner booth. Alex smoked and drank coffee as we waited for Marty to finish his hotdog. Tony and Jackie only had root beers.

"I always get the Chicago dog, too," Alex said as he looked around the restaurant. He seemed relaxed. He was on his own turf.

"Best I've ever had," I said generously.

Every now and then Marty would flick a glance at Tony or me. He wanted to know what had happened back there. Robbie Burns was something I hadn't told even Marty.

Mom and Dad never told us about him. Anything we learned about the undercover agent we learned at the bottom of the stairs. So Tony and I agreed we'd never tell anyone. Your dad's previous employment with the Mob is too good a subject to hold back from friends, even from acquaintances. But we never told about Robbie.

Which is why I wanted desperately to talk to Tony alone. It couldn't happen though because only Tony was big enough to handle Alex if he tried to get away. Which I didn't think would happen, but we couldn't chance it.

So to my chagrin, I realized I'd have to follow Tony's lead on this one.

"I ain't got all night, okay?" Alex said quietly.

Tony cleared his throat and thought a minute before he spoke. That's the difference between me and him. He thinks out what he says. I tumble it all out before it slips away from me.

"Alex, we need to know if you know anything about a . . . certain item. It was stolen from somebody, and we have to get it back. It's very important."

The light blue eyes narrowed. He leaned back and took a long pull on his cigarette, then opened his mouth in an O and puffed out a few smoke rings. I stared, fascinated. I'd never seen anybody do that. I watched as the rings floated past and got bigger and bigger, then dissolved into the air. Jackie coughed.

"I know a few things," he answered evasively. Then his expression darkened. "But I told you, I quit. Not gonna work for them anymore."

"What did you do for them?" Marty asked.

Alex shrugged. "Worked as a clerk behind the counter. Kind of the manager of the place. That was part of it. But they paid me good to keep an eye out for them too."

"An eye out for what?"

"People like you. Actually not like you, but people who'd come nosing around when they had no business to. I knew the people who could go upstairs." He looked at me, and for the first time I saw a trace of a smile. "You fooled me though. You were great." The admiration in his voice sent a warm flush up my cheeks. I covered for it by reaching for a napkin and blowing my nose.

"Why exactly are you quitting?" my brother asked.

"I told you. You may not believe me, but Burns is cool. At least he used to be. I wouldn't put anything past Kahlil, but when I opened the door to check on you and you weren't there, I didn't think anything of it 'cause Burns was upstairs. Then when Burns sent you down the stairs, laughing, and you looked like you did . . . I don't want no part of beating up little schoolgirls."

I sat up straight in indignation at his words. But Tony jumped in before I could protest.

"Alex, uh, back to this certain item. Do you know if—"

"Let's get something straight," Alex fired back in that quiet but firm voice. "I ain't gonna tell you nothing 'til you tell me why you'd let your sister barge in on a meeting with Ahmed Kahlil."

Tony held up his hands. "I didn't. I had no idea."

Alex glowered at him. "You idiots don't know who you're dealing with."

"We want to know. We need to know."

"Go back to where you came from. Forget about it."

"We *can't* forget," I said. "We *have* to get the carving back."

"The what?"

"A carving. Hair—uh, Burns stole it from someone we know."

"Might as well say good-bye to it then." Alex shrugged. "Burns don't give back nothing he steals. Why steal it then?"

How could I argue with such logic?

"You have to help us," Jackie pleaded, her brown eyes at their charming best.

"Why?" he answered flatly. A man of steel. Marty or Tony would have stood on the table and sang "The Star-spangled Banner" for her.

I looked at Alex Wendell and decided he needed a little enrichment in his life. A good old-fashioned story probably wouldn't kill him.

"You want to know why we want that carving so bad? All right, we'll tell you." I reached for Marty's root beer and took a long swig, then wiped my mouth with the back of my hand and began.

I started into the story at my dramatic best. I didn't play Anne Sullivan in *The Miracle Worker* for nothing. But school plays aside, I knew this had to be my very best performance. I only hoped I could tell it like Mr. Ten Brink.

Before I knew it, I forgot the theatrics and lived all over again the story of an orphaned Jewish boy found on a commuter train. I even described what Hans looked like, from my own mental portrait.

I told him about Gerrit, Rene, and even Katrina, the little girl who didn't want Hans to leave her. I told him about the fields of Andijk . . . flowers that blossomed in colors he had to see to believe. About Johann. About the friendship between Johann and the boy he knew as Kees. About a little wooden carving that meant the whole world to one young Dutch boy.

I told him about the day Uncle Gerrit came and how he and Kees walked away, and Johann waved and waved, held his carving and waved . . . and never saw him again.

"Wait, wait, wait—hold on . . . What do you mean he never saw him again?" Alex broke in anxiously.

I liked this kid.

Chapter Twelve

■

I FINISHED THE STORY AND LEFT NOTHING OUT. I EVEN TOLD HIM what I'd learned about Yad Vashem and the Avenue of the Righteous. I told him, convincingly I thought, that a tree belonged in the Ten Brinks' name among the others at the memorial.

Alex didn't say anything for a while. He flagged down a waitress to refill his coffee cup. We let him take his time. The ball was in his court.

At length, Alex sighed.

"So that's what this morning was all about. You're not with another gang in town. You're not some informant looking for dirt to sell to the cops."

I shook my head hard. "We just want the carving."

"Do you have any idea why they want it?" Marty asked.

"No. None of their business is mine. Kahlil would remind me of that a lot. They paid me to keep my eyes open, and that's it."

"Who *are* they, Alex?" Jackie asked.

Alex looked over at her, ready to answer the question, when he stopped and looked at her like he was seeing her for the first time.

"Hey . . . don't I know you?"

"I went to Hiawatha. I transferred to Beverly last year."

"Jackie . . . ?"

Jackie nodded and smiled. "D'Amico."

Tony smiled a little sheepishly. "Ah, I suppose we should introduce ourselves. I'm Tony DeWinter. That's Marty Behrens, and this is my sister Casey."

Alex flashed a grin, then made it disappear as if he'd been caught doing something he didn't normally do.

"Yeah, yeah. Nice to meet you. Not often I get ambushed in the street by the Brady Bunch."

We all laughed at that, and Alex joined in with a chuckle. He really seemed okay—once he loosened up.

"Your dad plays in a band, doesn't he?" Alex asked Jackie.

"Yes, he plays guitar in a band called Jericho."

Alex nodded. "I've heard him at the Selby Amphitheater a few times. He can wail."

I must have looked a little perplexed at his choice of words.

"It means he thinks Mr. D'Amico can play good," Tony explained to me on the side.

"Yeah, he's really got a rep. Word has it Death Warrant offered him a contract," Alex said, nodding. I looked at his T-shirt. It was the name of the band on his shirt and arm.

"They did," Jackie said. "But Dad wanted to play in a Christian band, so he started Jericho a few years ago. He's thinking about quitting his practice to go on the road."

"Nah, he don't want to do that," Alex said, then took a sip of his coffee. "He's also got a rep as a good lawyer. Got a few friends who think he's cool."

This was fun. Hip. Happening. We were chatting with a guy who knew what was cool and who could wail. A street dude who knew great hotdog joints. I was impressed.

"At least now I know why you charged into Kahlil's meeting room," Alex said to me. "You're stupid, but you've got guts."

Jackie repeated her earlier question. "Who are those guys, Alex?"

"Nobody to mess with."

"Yeah, we know. But maybe if we know who they are, we'll know why they want the carving."

"What's your point? I told you before, you can kiss your carving good-bye," Alex said. After he glanced at Jackie and me, he set down his cup and added, "Look, I'm sorry, okay? I really am. That Gerrit dude and his family deserve the tree. But when Kahlil wants something, he gets it. Don't matter how or why."

Alex looked around the restaurant. He looked behind him and to his side, then leaned a little toward us and spoke very quietly.

"Ahmed Kahlil is bad blood. His cousin is some big-time rich Arab guy who's wealthy from cocaine, not oil. Name is Claudio Muhtara."

I knew the kick I felt under the table came from Tony. Claudio Muhtara. The one Robbie Burns had spent years undercover trying to nail.

"Kahlil is Muhtara's connection for this whole half of the United States. My guess is, Muhtara's the one who wanted the carving. It just doesn't sound like Kahlil to mess with something so petty. Robbie Burns is Kahlil's right-hand man. Carries out a lot of orders. That's why he was the one to steal it."

"How did he know Mr. Ten Brink had it?" Marty asked.

Alex shrugged. "You said the Israeli Embassy knew about it. Muhtara has connections everywhere."

My stomach lurched. This thing got scarier all the time.

"We've got to get it back before it gets to Muhtara."

Tony said it quietly but with such resolve, it made me sit up a little straighter. Weren't we Classifieds? Righters of wrong? Doers of good? Helpers of mankind?

"You guys have lost your brains," Alex muttered as he shook his head.

"Help us, Alex," Tony urged.

I expected him to laugh or say something like, "Later, losers." He didn't. He just closed his eyes while he shook his head and gave a little snort.

"It's perfect," Marty said eagerly. "They don't know you quit, so don't. You can sneak upstairs and steal it before they know what hit 'em. They'll never know it was you."

Alex looked at Marty like he needed a head transplant. "Tell me how I'm supposed to do this, Double-Oh-Seven. I've never been up there before. I don't even know where to look."

"*I* do." The three guys looked at me, then resumed their conversation.

"If they find out, I'm history," Alex said.

"They won't. You look like an expert," Tony replied.

"At *what*?" Alex shot back.

"I said I know where to find it. Let me do it," I persisted.

"You're not going up there again," Alex snapped. "If anyone does, I do. You just have to tell me where to look."

No one spoke for a moment.

Alex groaned as he messed up his hair with both hands. Then he looked at us tiredly.

"If we do it, we do it tonight. I saw them both leave this afternoon, and they didn't carry anything with them, so it must still be there."

"This can be, like, your initiation! Then you can be a part of our new agency," Marty said with a sparkle.

"What agency?" Alex asked warily.

"The Classifieds. We're a brand-new organization. Only we're so new, we haven't figured out yet what we're all about."

"We have so," I replied indignantly. "We help people who don't necessarily ask for it but who more or less deserve it. That's our creed, sort of."

"Oh yeah?" Alex replied icily. "And what makes you the judge of who deserves help and who doesn't?"

I felt like he'd slapped me. I stared at him—but I knew he was right. My cheeks grew hot, and I tried to stammer out an answer."

"I—I guess I didn't mean it that way. It's just—Mr. Ten Brink isn't an easy guy to get along with and—"

"Whether they do or don't deserve it should have nothing to do with it. If people need help, they need help. No matter who. No matter what," Alex stated less icily.

We all looked at each other while Alex poured cream into his coffee.

"I guess you just rewrote our creed," Tony mumbled with a half-smile. "We just want to be as much help as we can."

"Now *that* I can drink to," Alex said as he lifted his cup in salute.

I smiled at Alex, amazed. This was the creepy kid who had glared at us from behind a candy counter? I never would have believed he'd turn out this way. With convictions.

"But hey," Jackie said, "we shouldn't consider what he's going to do as an initiation. That wouldn't be fair. *We* didn't have to go through an initiation."

"I don't want no part of no stupid club," Alex growled. "I do this thing tonight and that's it, okay? As it is, I'm going to have to work for them longer. Once they find the carving gone and then I quit too—"

"They'd know you did it, and they'd come after you," I finished for him.

Alex stared moodily into his cup. I couldn't think of a single thing to say. No one could.

Alex finally pushed his coffee cup away from him. "Well, let's get it over with. Julian is working right now. I'll tell him I have to use the john or something. To make sure he doesn't hear me walking around upstairs, you guys can distract him. I'm sure you won't have a problem with that," he added with a sideways glance at me.

I pulled a few wadded dollar bills out of my pocket to pay for the bill, wondering how much of a tip I should leave. I usually do McDonald's. I left what I felt was a healthy fifty-cent tip, and we all headed for the door.

I tried to thank Alex for his help. "Hey, Alex, we just want to say thanks. If there's anything—"

He wheeled sharply around and stared me dead in the eye. I stepped back reflexively.

"Let's get something straight," he hissed with a return to his former creepiness, "I ain't doin' this for you or any of your friends."

He pulled away from me. Despite his rudeness, I smiled. He didn't have to tell me who he was doing it for. I already knew.

■ ■ ■

I checked my watch as we entered the store. 8:33 P.M. Alex had gone in two minutes earlier so Julian wouldn't know we were together. I told Alex exactly where to find the carving. Barring any unforeseen complications—like a locked door—and giving time for the bathroom bit, Alex should be in and out in four minutes.

To make it look good, Tony suggested with a pink flare on

his cheeks that we act like we're couples. Boyfriends and girl-friends. We're out having a good time, on our way to a concert, and we get the munchies and drop in to grab some junk food. It made sense; I thought it was a great idea. Tony caught Jackie's hand in his, and the pink hue deepened to red. Jackie blushed too and looked away with a little smile. I rolled my eyes and snatched Marty's hand. Big deal.

The store didn't seem as dimly lit as earlier today, at least in contrast with the darkening skies outside. A kid with brownish-red, curly hair was stocking a shelf next to the counter with candy bars. He seemed much more the type to work in a candy store—slightly pudgy with an air of efficiency. A man who knew his candy.

I wondered if he even knew what the upstairs room was used for. He acknowledged us with a nod and a greeting-type smile. Definitely not the hood type. I was getting to be somewhat of an expert on hoods.

"Uh, you want anything, *honey*?" Tony asked Jackie a bit too loudly.

"Oh, uh, let's see if they have any Gummi Bears, *babe*," Jackie answered.

I fought back a nearly overpowering desire to laugh hysterically.

"The Gummi Bears are over there in the glass decanters," Julian said helpfully, pointing with a chubby finger. "We also have Gummi sharks, worms, rats, lizards, spiders, and golf balls. Just scoop it into a bag, and I'll weigh it at the counter."

"Thanks," Tony said.

I heard a muffled thud but couldn't identify it.

"Hey," Marty half-yelled, "got any of those red twisty things—oh, what do you call them . . . ?"

Julian gave him a funny look. "Licorice?"

"Yeah, that's it!"

"He really loves licorice," I explained loudly.

"I really love licorice. Especially when it's red and, uh, twisty." Even I winced at that. I squeezed Marty's hand hard. This hand-holding business was getting icky. Marty's hands sweat when he's nervous.

"The licorice is over here . . ." Julian gestured toward a rack below the one he was stocking. I pulled my hand away from Marty's slimy hold and wiped it on my jeans.

"I'm going to look at the boxes of candy, sweetie pie," I said and turned away.

"Take your time, uh, my little dumpling," Marty answered.

I stared for the second time that day into a box of anemic chocolates. I lifted packages, examined prices, pretended to be absorbed in the candy. *It shouldn't be taking this long,* I thought anxiously as the Chicago dog started up round one with my hamburger and fries. I looked at my watch. 8:38. Five minutes already! Where was Alex? If the door was locked, he would have come back down already.

I risked a glance at Tony. He and Jackie lifted lids and laughed and joked. Marty was now genuinely interested not in the pack of licorice tucked under his arm, but in a fistful of baseball card packs he had picked up. He and Julian chatted eagerly about cards and players.

More customers came into the store, a bunch of kids our own age who looked as normal as we did. Probably on their way to a concert and they got the munchies, I thought. They laughed like hyenas about something or other. Just when it died down, a girl in their group burped, and they all began laughing again.

I looked again at Tony and Jackie. Oblivious to the world. I should have seen it coming.

"No kidding!" I heard Marty say. "You've got a *signed*

Bruno Haley? From the minors? I'm sick. I'm absolutely sick. Bruno Haley!"

I sighed impatiently. The little store seemed more crowded now. My watch said 8:40.

I strode casually to the hallway door, humming and poking at various items along my way, then opened the door just wide enough to slip through. I shut it, leaving the noisy store behind me.

I crept along in the narrow corridor, my heart pumping furiously, my nose tingling like sparks were about to fly from it. Behind me I heard another eruption of wild laughter.

A thump overhead made me jump and gasp. Then came a series of thumps, thuds, scrapings. Then silence. The silence was worse.

I whipped around and stared at the door to the store. *Tony? Marty? What should I do?* I turned back to the stairway, then sprang to the foot of the stairs and stared upward. After a second's hesitation I took the steps two at a time, then stood in front of the door, more scared than I'd ever been before.

The door stood ajar. I didn't hear anything except the slamming of my heart. Far away and below I heard laughter.

"Alex?" I whispered.

I put a hand on the door and eased it open a few inches. There was no light—just a dirty glow from the window. I couldn't see a thing. I stepped into the room.

"Alex? Where are you?"

I heard a weird garbling sound, then a choked cry. "Run, Casey!"

Whumpf! Something from behind the door knocked me off my feet and onto my rear. Pain shrieked in my side. When I started to scramble up, someone threw on a light. I looked up to see Ahmed Kahlil towering over me, baseball bat in hand.

Rage disfigured his ugly face into something I didn't want to stick around to contemplate. I sprang sideways for the door. Ahmed raised the bat and lunged for me.

Something suddenly roared and plowed into me, and I plowed into Kahlil. We crashed to the floor, and I fought to get untangled from black leather and flailing arms and legs. One arm snaked around my neck, and my breath was cut off in an instant. I gasped and clutched my throat as I kicked wildly, then broke away.

I saw Robbie Burns and Ahmed Kahlil fight in a vicious, writhing blur.

Gunshot!

One of them slumped still, but I couldn't tell which. And I didn't wait to find out. I held my side and made for the door.

Then came a roar of fury, followed by a bone-crushing grip. Kahlil snagged me and swung me around like a discus. I shot across the room—straight for a wall. I slammed into it, and as I slid to the floor, I heard someone call my name . . . heard a far-off burst of group laughter . . . saw a bundle of cracked brown leather.

Darkness descended, muffling everything into nothing.

Chapter Thirteen

■

I DREAMED ABOUT THE TIME MY DAD CAME HOME FROM A GOLFING trip with an insect bite on the side of his nose. It was red and puffed up like a giant, lumpy cheese ball. It looked funny, but honestly my dad was in misery. It closed off his sinus passages, so he had to breathe out of his mouth. He walked around with his mouth hanging open and his nose casting a bigger shadow than his head.

I dreamed other things too. I was a leaf in the wind, tossed and flipped and whooshed around. I like those flying kind of dreams. You dip like you're going to bottom out, then swoop up in a sudden rush and soar to the sky.

Then Casey the Leaf turned into a gangster wielding a baseball bat autographed by Bruno Haley. Except the gangster was really me on the inside, though nobody knew.

Then things got uncomfortable. People began to bug me. I had distant flashes of faces peering down at me. Pokes, prods, pain. I tried to fight back with the baseball bat, but it felt as if it were made of iron. So I just clung to it and closed my eyes tight and wished all the people away.

I smelled peppermint-gum breath and felt the whispery touch of a kiss on my forehead. I sighed, and the dreams disappeared.

▪ ▪ ▪

Pain woke me. I groaned weakly, my No Pain Policy up in arms. I lay with my eyes shut, trying to locate the sources of discomfort. My side. Definitely my side. And my face. All over my face. My shoulder.

After a few fluttering tries—my lids felt like garbage can tops—I held my eyes open long enough to see what looked like a remote control to a TV. It hooked into a stand. Next to the stand was my mom, curled up in a chair, dozing. That glance proved to be exertion enough, and I fell asleep again.

▪ ▪ ▪

Low tones, a soft chuckle. My dad. I smiled. Couldn't seem to wake up though. Didn't matter. I felt better.

▪ ▪ ▪

I woke with perfect clarity. At last. No more hazy, sleepy stuff. I opened my eyes. Mom and Dad sat in two chairs near the bed. Dad had his head back on the seat, his eyes closed, his mouth slightly open. He was snoring. Mom was reading her Bible. She sat near enough that I could tell where she read from—the Psalms. Her favorites.

"Cribbage anyone?" I croaked.

Mom jumped and poked Dad in the side. She broke into a beautiful smile and leaned toward me. She traced a finger down my cheek, tears filling her eyes.

"Hi, sweetheart."

"Hi, Mom," I whispered hoarsely.

"So much for my makeup job, eh?" she joked as a tear trickled down her face. She wiped it away quickly and smiled.

"Aw, she's still beautiful," Dad said as his smiling face

appeared next to Mom's. His brown eyes were both relieved and tired. His laugh lines seemed to stand out more. He needed a shave. I like it when he looks like he needs a shave.

"You guys are a sight for sore eyes, and I mean that literally," I muttered as I reached up and gingerly touched a puffy eye. My nose had tape over it, and I wondered if it was broken.

"So what's the damage report?" I asked.

"Well, we have an engine core leak, a hull breach, and we've lost decks 6, 7, and 8. But the shields are still holding, and with any luck we can be up to warp speed, in, oh, about—"

"Phil, will you stop?" Mom interrupted, poking his arm.

I managed a grin. Then, for the first time, I thought about Alex. And Robbie. And Kahlil. Mom and Dad stopped smiling when they saw the expression on my face.

Dad patted Mom's arm. "Honey, why don't you let Dr. Scott or one of the nurses know Casey's awake. And maybe you should make a call or two."

Mom nodded. After a smile at me and a squeeze on my arm, she left the room. I watched her leave, then looked at Dad. He moved closer to me, sat in Mom's chair, and just held my hand.

"What time is it?" I asked. "What *day* is it?"

Dad looked at his watch. "It's 3:15 P.M. Sunday."

"*Sunday?*" Wow. The last time I looked at my watch, it was 8:40 Saturday.

Dad didn't seem too talkative. He wanted me to start first. That's usually how it goes with me and my dad. He waits for me to come out with whatever's bothering me or whatever's on my mind. Normally that's not a problem. But this time I didn't know where to begin.

I was afraid to ask about Robbie. About Alex. I thought I'd start with something easier.

"Did I break anything?" I asked hopefully.

The scourge of a tomboy childhood is to live through it without breaking so much as a pinkie. Friends boasted of broken arms or legs in casts for months. But I had only three stitches on my thumb where I snagged it while baiting a fishhook. A pathetic testament to the life of a rugged adventurer.

Dad gave a low chuckle. "You broke three ribs and suffered a concussion. They thought you broke your nose, but it only got a good wallop."

I relaxed, satisfied. I could leave the hospital in dignity. All this pain didn't go for nothing. A *concussion*. Now *there's* something to discuss in the locker room after gym class. "Yep. Broke three ribs. Smashed 'em to bits. But the real danger was the *concussion*. Doctors never saw such an awful one. Nearly killed me . . ."

"Dad, what exactly is a concussion?"

"Well, it's when you've received a blow to the head, and the brain ends up with what is usually temporarily impaired functioning. Your brain made you sort of shut down to, uh, regroup."

"Like it took a vacation?"

"Exactly."

I didn't want to ask him. I wanted to stick to the easy stuff for the rest of my life. But I had to know. I closed my eyes and again heard the gunshot and saw the limp body.

"Is Robbie Burns dead?"

"No."

"Alex?"

"He's fine. He's in a room down the hall."

I released my breath. "Then who got shot?"

"A man by the name of Ahmed Kahlil. He's dead."

I was very, very tired all of a sudden. They could explain later how a shot man managed to hurl me across a room.

"Dad," I whispered as my eyelids sank, "I don't mean to be rude . . ."

He kissed my forehead. "Sleep, child."

▪ ▪ ▪

My No Pain Policy, outraged and indignant, rapped on the door to my brain and demanded action. I roused from a sound sleep to an ache more insistent than any I'd ever felt. My right side felt permanently wrecked. Any fraction of movement detonated explosions of agony. Even before consciousness completely swept in, I moaned for morphine.

Someone in the room pressed the buzzer to summon a nurse, and through a blur of misery I saw a white, plump angel of mercy bustle into the room and stick a hypodermic needle into my rear. In seconds the pain vanished, and I blinked awake.

Tony grinned at me. "Hi, Morning Breath."

"That bad?"

"Yep. Here . . ." He unwrapped a cherry Lifesaver and popped it into my mouth.

"You look terrible. Your eye looks really cool."

"Thanks. Do you have a mirror?"

"Yeah, but I'm supposed to ask if you want any water first."

"Please."

He poured water from a pitcher into a Styrofoam cup and stuck a bent straw into it. I didn't realize how thirsty I was.

"Holy cow. I didn't know broken ribs felt this bad."

Tony pushed my legs slightly to the side and sat down on

the bed. "I know how you feel. I broke a couple my first year on the football team. Worst part is, there's nothing to show for your pain."

"You mean I don't get a cast?"

"Nope. They usually tape your ribs for support, but that's it."

"I couldn't break something *normal*, like a wrist," I complained.

"Just be glad you got out of there alive."

Before I could ask him what on earth happened after Kahlil used me for horseshoe practice, we heard a tap at the door.

"Come on in," Tony said over his shoulder.

In came Alex Wendell, moving rather slowly and sporting the latest in hospital fashion wear. I probably looked just as cute, I realized as I glanced down at my gown. At least it didn't have little bears all over it like when I had my appendix out.

I smiled at Alex but discovered my smile couldn't lift very high. It pushed up my cheeks, which made my eye and nose crinkle, which didn't feel too cool.

Alex studied me critically, then gave a low whistle. "Looks like you had a date with a steamroller."

I studied him right back and noticed for the first time the freshly plastered cast on his right arm. It even covered the tattoo on his bicep.

"Baseball bat?" I asked.

He nodded and asked, "Wall? I didn't see it, but I heard it."

"Yeah, wall. He also clobbered me with the bat the second I came into the room. Broke three ribs." It was the first time I got to tell someone, and his response satisfied me. He winced and held a hand to his own side in sympathy.

"No fun. I didn't break any, but I bruised some when I was ten. It killed."

Tony pushed a chair toward Alex, and he sat down. Other than the cast and the new hospital garb, Alex didn't look any different. But he *seemed* different. Normal. Relaxed, unafraid, and plain old normal.

"You have to tell me what happened," I said as I plumped a few pillows around me and settled in for a great story. "You too, Tony. I want to know every single detail."

"Maybe we should wait until Jackie and Marty get here," Tony replied uncertainly.

"No way!"

"Or maybe we should wait until Robbie comes," Alex said to Tony. "I guess he and the other local feds want to talk to us. The doctors and our parents wouldn't let them last night. They said they'd come back tonight."

"Local feds?" I asked.

Alex got up and peeked into the hallway, then shut the door to the room. He sat back down, his bright blue eyes sparkling with eagerness.

"Yeah. You're not gonna believe this. I found out last night that *Robbie Burns is really an undercover fed.*"

Our reaction—or lack thereof—didn't please him.

"A *fed*, you guys—*FBI!*" he implored. He looked from me to Tony, desperate for a suitable response. Tony looked at me, and we both couldn't help laughing a little.

"Alex, we know. We knew yesterday when you talked with us in the street, right after you mentioned his name."

"Huh? How did you know? I've known Robbie for six years, and I never knew."

"Well—"

"Wait . . . It's that gang of yours, right? The Classifieds. You guys work with the government or something?"

"No—nothing like that. We only formed that club yesterday," I said. I could hardly believe my own words. Only yesterday? I'd packed enough living into yesterday to last a whole six months!

"Then how . . . ?"

"It's a long story," I said with a glance at Tony. He met my eyes and nodded.

"See, a long time ago my dad used to be in the Mob," I said, then paused. But this time Alex didn't react. I should have known. Organized crime was nothing new with him. "Anyway, to make this short, Robbie contacted him and got him to work with the government to bring down a big-time mobster— Hernando Giminez. Ever hear of him?"

"Oh yeah. Who hasn't? *Your dad* helped bring him down?"

"Yep. He and a few others."

"Wow. Kahlil did a lot of business with Giminez."

"So that's how we knew about Robbie. Though actually we weren't supposed to know. We sort of found out by, ah, accident." I paused and let Alex absorb that. But not for long. It was time for *me* to get some answers.

"Okay, guys," I told Tony and Alex sternly as I reached for my Styrofoam cup, "start talking. And don't leave a single detail out."

Chapter
Fourteen

■

As TONY SIGNED ALEX'S CAST WITH A BIG BLACK MARKER, ALEX began his story.

• • •

Saturday, May 5. 8:33 P.M.

Alex checked his watch as he entered the store. He'd just told us it shouldn't take him more than four minutes to retrieve the stolen statue. He told us to come into the store after two minutes.

Alex nodded at Julian as he walked toward the hallway door.

Julian looked at him in surprise. "What are *you* doing here?"

"Going to a concert at the Selby Amphitheater. Have to use the john."

Julian tried to say something, but Alex ignored him and went his way, closing the door behind him. He crept down the hallway.

I guess I had told the story of the carving pretty good. In fact, it got on Alex's nerves when I tried a little too hard to sell him on it. But he bought it the minute I told him Gerrit picked up the skinny Jewish kid. That immediately reminded him of someone who gave *him* a chance when no one else would.

He only hoped that certain someone wasn't upstairs right now. Or on his way here. Robbie often showed up when least expected.

Robbie got Alex the job here, managing a candy store instead of running packages for no-goods on the street. Robbie told Alex about a band called Jericho. Robbie introduced Alex to Chris D'Amico, lead guitarist for Jericho and the lawyer who helped his mother place a restraining order on Alex's heavy-drinking father. Robbie also sent a white-faced girl with a freshly bloodied lip down the back stairs.

One thing Alex's mom always tried to teach him: be true to yourself, no matter what. Without Kahlil around, Robbie was cool. He tried to help people. He respected people. But with Kahlil in the picture, Robbie changed. Got almost as moody as Ahmed. Acted like he didn't give a hoot whether Alex lived or died. Robbie wasn't true to himself, whichever self that was.

Alex stood at the foot of the stairs and remembered the anger he'd felt just that morning. Anger as he watched the spunky kid he knew now as Casey slink down the stairs while Robbie Burns laughed his head off.

Even after Jackie and I had left, Alex stood a long while and stared up at the door. Robbie had helped Alex and his family more times than he could remember. He owed a lot to Robbie Burns. He cared about Robbie. More than he ever cared about his own father.

But Robbie wasn't someone Alex could respect. Not someone so two-faced. Act one way around one group of people, then totally different around someone else. Just so Kahlil would keep him as his Number One. So he could wear the gold chains and diamond earrings, act like a high and mighty big shot.

Alex would rather be like Gerrit Ten Brink.

The man put it all on the line for one little kid, even though the Nazis could've blown Gerrit's brains out for it. Gerrit put more on the line than his own life; he risked the lives of his entire family for someone he didn't even know. Gerrit was true to himself.

Alex started softly up the stairs. He couldn't remember Burns or Kahlil ever taking a key from their pockets to open the door. Hopefully it was unlocked.

He reached the top of the stairs and breathed a sigh of relief when he saw no light under the door. He tried the door— it wasn't locked. He swung it silently forward and peered into the darkness.

I had told him the carving was under the coffee table by the couch. He made out the dark shapes of furniture in the feeble light coming through the window, light from a neon sign above the party store next door. As his eyes adjusted to the dark, he suddenly realized the chair was bulkier than a chair was supposed to be. He stopped short.

Ahmed Kahlil.

"I've been waiting for you." The chilling voice broke the silence.

Alex always hated to hear Kahlil talk. The voice sounded like it belonged to the cold dampness at the bottom of a well.

"Got friends at Delbert's," it grated on mercilessly. "Called me five minutes ago. Said you talked to the kid who came for the carving today."

Alex began an inch by inch retreat toward the door.

"I don't tolerate disloyalty. Even from nothings like you."

Kahlil rose from the chair. Against the soft neon glow Alex saw the outline of the baseball bat Kahlil carried. He thumped it against his leg as he moved slowly toward Alex.

"What do you have to say for yourself, you pathetic waste of time?" Kahlil rasped with stiff lips.

When Alex broke for the door, the bat shot through the air. Pain exploded in his arm, and Kahlil tackled him and dragged him to the ground. He struggled and twisted and tried to get a punch at Kahlil, but the older man pinned him to the floor with one arm and reached for the baseball bat with the other.

With a vicious snarl, Kahlil lifted the bat in the air, ready to crush Alex's skull. From nowhere a hairy-knuckled hand stopped the downswing.

"Not Alex, Kahlil," Robbie grunted as he whipped an arm around the man's neck and dragged him off of Alex.

There was a scuffle, muffled grunts, curses, the sound of connected punches, a surprised yelp of rage. Then silence.

Alex hugged his hurt arm with the other and rocked back and forth in pain. He sat still when the neon glow revealed not Burns but Kahlil rising in front of him. Kahlil stood, breathing hard, and stared down at Burns. Then he turned to Alex.

Alex could not see his enemy's eyes in the dimness. He didn't have to. He could feel the waves of hate the minute Kahlil turned toward him.

Alex groaned, partly from pain, partly from fear, and scrabbled backward on the floor until he hit the wall. In two long, quick strides Kahlil reached Alex. He grabbed him by his shirt front and yanked him up to his face.

"Now look what you made me do," he hissed.

Steps sounded on the stairs, and Kahlil clapped a hand over Alex's mouth. Alex bit down deeply and over Kahlil's curse yelled, "Run, Casey!" Kahlil flung Alex to the floor, snatched his bat, and leveled a blow at the intruder—me.

Alex made a helpless attempt to get to his feet, but pain and fear held him back. So he whispered the only prayer he knew.

"Oh, God . . ."

A gunshot sounded.

■ ■ ■

I didn't even notice when a nurse brought my dinner tray. Not until Alex stopped and lifted the lid on my entree with interest, then frowned.

"I'd rather have a Chicago dog, with plenty of chips."

I stared at the neat square of lasagna. My mom's lasagna is sloppy and probably tastes a whole lot better.

"I don't remember anything after hitting the wall. What happened?"

Tony and Alex exchanged a look.

"You don't remember *anything*?" Tony asked.

"No," I replied suspiciously, darting a glance at each of them. "Why?"

Tony hopped off the bed and got comfortable in the recliner. He hiked up his feet on the metal bed frame.

"Looks like it's time for me to take over."

■ ■ ■

Saturday, May 5. 8:39 P.M.

Tony realized he probably didn't need to hold Jackie's hand while they inspected the Gummi worms. He didn't mind though.

He'd seen Jackie several times at our house, hanging out with me. He'd say hi to her in the hallway at school and even chatted with her a few times at Honor Society meetings. She was my friend—just another pipsqueak freshman at Hamilton High. Until that day in the candy store.

He looked down at the pretty, brown-eyed girl with the

light brown hair pulled back in a ponytail. This detective stuff wasn't so bad.

Jackie chatted about weird candy. "Ever have those wax bottle things with the gross-tasting juice inside?"

"I used to eat the bottles."

"Yuck!" She grinned and made a face, then pointed to another display. "I used to get that stuff in my stocking every year. The problem is, you'd eat just as much of the paper as the little candy dots."

Jackie smiled at Tony, and his heart made a strange jump. He wondered if he should kiss her, just to make all this look really authentic. After all, real boyfriends and girlfriends do that kind of stuff in public every now and then. This was all theatrics and shoot, he'd wanted to be an actor since he was a kid. A kiss wouldn't kill him, after all . . .

Tony suddenly pulled in a sharp breath and jerked his hand away from Jackie to look at his watch. 8:43. He sent a fast glance around the store. Where was Casey? Marty was talking with Julian. A bunch of kids laughed and joked.

"Marty . . ." Tony called softly.

Marty looked his way, talking all the while to Julian. He held up his hand as if to say, "Yeah, yeah, just a minute" and jabbered on. The group of laughing kids roared over something in the display case.

"Marty!" Tony growled between his teeth.

Marty snapped his attention back to Tony, who pointed at his watch. For the first time Marty remembered their mission. He looked at his own watch, then stared in bewilderment at Tony. He looked around the store. *Where's Casey?* he mouthed.

Tony shook his head and shrugged as a ripple of apprehension flooded through his stomach. He scowled and glanced at the door to the side of the counter. It would be just like Casey to—

Boom!

A small explosion above the ceiling silenced the entire store. Tony froze. Blood drained from his face in an instant. He started automatically for the door. A solid *thud* from somewhere above rattled the display case windows.

Tony burst through the door and pounded down the hallway with Marty at his heels. Somebody following them turned on a light, illuminating a stairway bottom. Tony charged up the steps. But before he reached the top, a man staggered out of the room clutching his stomach.

Tony halted without warning, and Marty banged into him. Both boys watched in horror as the man stopped and swayed. Wild eyes stared unseeingly at Tony. Then the man toppled forward.

Tony yelled and yanked Marty against the wall as Ahmed Kahlil tumbled past them. Vaguely, sounding like it was a mile away, Tony heard screams and a commotion at the bottom of the stairs. The noise died to one single thought, one name pounding with Tony's every heartbeat. *Casey . . . Casey . . . Casey . . .*

He mechanically continued up the stairs.

He stopped in the doorway, seeing a man in an unmoving pile on his right and Alex Wendell sagged against a wall on his left. But he focused only on the place where I lay curled next to a coffee table. He ran to kneel beside me and pulled my shoulder toward him.

"Casey . . ." His voice trembled as he reached out to touch my face. His hands moved in helpless gestures, then he turned ferociously on Marty.

"Call 9-1-1!" he screamed. "Now!"

Marty stared at me for a second, his breath coming in ragged gasps. Then he turned on his heel and flew down the stairs.

I moaned slightly. Tony brushed my hair back, sickened at the damp feel of blood. Then he saw for the first time what lay cradled in my arms.

A brown, cracked leather bundle.

■ ■ ■

"The baseball bat!" I shrieked. "I dreamed I was holding a baseball bat!"

"I watched you crawl over to the table after you hit the wall," Alex said quietly. "Once you had the carving, you didn't move again."

I shook my head in amazement. I didn't remember any of this. I stared at Alex and Tony.

"Where is it?" I said in a voice that sounded tinny and far-away. "Where's the carving?"

Something odd was happening between Alex and Tony. Tony glowered at him, and Alex wouldn't meet his eye. Or mine.

At that moment, a tap sounded at the door, and Robbie Burns walked in.

Chapter Fifteen

∎

*A*LEX WAS ON HIS FEET AS FAST AS THE AWKWARD BALANCE OF HIS new cast allowed. He faced Robbie defiantly, a contemptuous sneer on his face.

"I need to talk to you," Robbie Burns the FBI Guy said to us all, with no trace of Robbie Burns the Gangster. "It seems we have a lot to discuss."

He had a butterfly bandage on one eye and a cut in the center of a puffy lower lip. He moved to the other side of the bed a little slowly, and I wondered what Kahlil had done to him.

He eased into a chair with a protective hand over his ribs, and I suddenly remembered the slit in Kahlil's boot that housed a wicked-looking knife.

"It's nice we can officially meet," Robbie said warmly with his hand outstretched to me. I shook it, vaguely bewildered. "My name is Robbie Burns. Special agent with the Federal Bureau of Investigation."

Calm, kind of businesslike, and definitely normal. A pleasant voice. He was even kind of handsome for an older guy (he had to be at least thirty), which is strange because he wasn't handsome before.

I studied him as he looked alternately at the three of us—

me on the bed, Tony next to me in the recliner, and Alex standing near the door like he was ready to leave.

I watched him as he looked at Alex. I saw a funny mix of sadness and regret in the amber eyes. And pain.

"I need to talk to you too, Alex," he said quietly.

"I ain't got nothin' to say to you!"

"I told you last night who I really am. There wasn't any time to tell you the rest."

"You're a traitor!" Alex shouted as he jabbed the air with a finger pointed at Robbie. "The rest don't matter."

The agent's eyes dropped to look at the floor.

"I never meant to hurt you, Alex. You must understand my position."

"I understand plenty. You didn't trust me. All that time, all we've been through, and you didn't trust me," Alex hissed, his voice tightening. He fought to keep from crying. "If you just would have *told* me, maybe I could have handled it the time you said to Kahlil I wasn't worth the smog I breathed."

"He was looking for that kind of response, Alex. Please, please understand. Don't you see? He treated you like dirt, and I had to agree with everything he did."

"You're still a traitor," Alex ground out between bared teeth. "You could have trusted me, and you know it."

He jerked open the door and left.

Robbie released a heavy sigh, and no one said anything for a while.

"He's right," he finally muttered.

I heard defeat in those words, and my underdog mentality leapt to reply.

"Hey, you're a *good* guy. He should be happy to realize it because I know Alex is a good guy himself."

Robbie smiled a little, but it faded fast. "I don't expect you to understand, Casey. My superiors are up in arms, Alex thinks I'm the jerk I pretended to be, and I feel like someone stuffed me in a garbage disposal and flipped the switch. It hasn't been a banner week for this good guy."

"You too?" I asked sympathetically. I pointed to my side and nodded. "Baseball bat."

Robbie pointed to a spot below his chest. "Knife."

"How many stitches?"

"Twenty. Fortunately, the stab wasn't deep. How many stitches on your eye?"

I touched the bandage that covered half my eye. "None. Just a gash."

We looked at each other, and then Robbie smiled crookedly and displayed a glimpse of his superb teeth. I smiled gingerly back.

"Like father, like daughter," Robbie said, shaking his head.

"I know your work is top secret and all that," Tony commented, "but can't you tell us why on earth you wanted the carving in the first place?"

Robbie rubbed his face and looked at us tiredly. "I can't."

"We *have* to know," I said testily. "I didn't break bones for nothing."

He shook his head. "You don't know what you're asking, Casey. This is highly classified material."

"I won't tell a soul," I said. To reassure him I added, "They can stick thorns under my nails, hang me by my toes, make me eat raw liver, and burn Starr Cassidy books right in front of my face, but no sir, I'll not say a word. Not even if they put fleas in my hair or—"

"He's got the picture, Casey!" Tony snapped.

I suddenly gasped. "What about Marty and Jackie? They'll

have to know too. They're Classifieds, and they've been in on this from the start."

"Haven't you been listening to a single word I've said?" Robbie asked, and I could tell he was getting ticked off. "I can't tell you."

"Then why are you here?"

"Two reasons. To get the carving back and to tell you to give up on it."

"Never," I replied simply. Give the carving back, end of story. Yeah, right. In a pig's eye.

"You tell us why you want it so bad, and I'll tell you why it's impossible to give it back."

Robbie snorted. "I already know. I talked to that redhaired kid last night."

"Marty! That weasel! We're supposed to be a *secret* helper agency."

"Don't blame Marty," Tony said. "It's not his fault."

"Can't you understand?" I pleaded with the agent. "Hans is dead; only the carving can prove to the investigators at Yad Vashem what Mr. Ten Brink's family did. It's the only thing that's going to put a tree on the Avenue of the Righteous. Besides that, the carving is the *single most important posses-sion* to old Mr. Ten Brink. It means Hans. It means heroes. It reminds him of what's *important*. Can't you see that?"

Robbie closed his eyes. "Don't make my job any harder than it is, Casey. This is without doubt the most confounded case I've ever been assigned to. Would it make it any easier if I said that giving the carving back to me is a matter of life and death?"

"Whose life or death?" Tony asked.

"Come on, Tony, I can't answer that," Robbie replied wearily.

We were at an impasse. How could I (or Alex, really) give

back the carving when it meant so much to the old teacher?
I looked at my hands as the silence in the room grew uncomfortable.

"Mr. Burns," my brother began carefully, "it might make
a difference if we knew why you want the carving so bad. Tell
us why and it's *possible* we could arrive at a decision to give
it back. We are reasonable."

The agent's eyes narrowed. "That's bribery," he answered
coldly. "The FBI doesn't negotiate with kids."

"The way I see it, you don't have a choice," Tony replied
just as coldly. "Toss us in jail for not giving back the carving.
Go ahead. But tell us what we want to know and you'll have
a greater chance to get it back."

Oh, did I love this. Tony could play hardball like a pro. I
silently cheered him on as the two of them glared at each other.

"It's still bribery," Robbie said, but with a note of concession in his tone.

"It's an exchange."

"A *possible* exchange," I reminded them.

"You should be an agent," Robbie told my brother.

Tony shrugged. "I want to be an actor."

Robbie's face darkened as he looked at the door. Where
Alex had stood. "That's part of the job. Being an actor."

He borrowed one of my pillows and tucked it in by his side.
He propped one leg up on the bed frame like Tony had done,
then winced as he lifted the other one up. I could relate. It
seemed like any movement at all triggered pain in my ribs.

After Robbie settled in, he began his story.

■ ■ ■

"I've been an agent for eight years now, the last six undercover.
We've been working with the CIA and the Mossad, the Israeli

secret service, to establish connections with a man named Claudio Xavier Muhtara. Only connections. That's how I came to be associated with Ahmed Rashid Kahlil.

"Kahlil was distantly related to Muhtara, and because of that he was the Number One for Hernando Giminez." He paused to look at us significantly. We nodded. Yeah, we knew the guy.

"After your dad and a few others helped us take down Giminez, Kahlil moved into position as—I guess you'd call it Godfather—for this area. Trouble was, he didn't have Giminez's aptitudes for criminal activity."

"Could've fooled me," I said with feeling.

"I mean for sophisticated, white-collar criminal activity. On international levels. Kahlil was a common thug. Trained only to intimidate, to protect Giminez, and to kill. He didn't have the brains to pick up where Giminez left off. Not for money laundering or networking with businesses in other localities. I worked to keep Kahlil in the graces of Muhtara. If Muhtara dumped him—relative or not—I'd lose my contact."

"*How* did you keep him in Muhtara's graces?" Tony asked.

Robbie shrugged a bit sheepishly. "I just made suggestions to Ahmed about ways to increase productivity. Ways to keep the ball rolling. Ahmed would pass it on to Muhtara, claiming the ideas as his own of course, and things went fine."

I stared at this man. This Christian who pointed my dad in God's direction.

"Not long ago," he continued, placing his hand over his knife wound, "my superior contacted me, frantic about the possibility of an agent in the Middle East losing his cover. Seems this agent's father had previously set about locating a man named Johann Ten Brink."

"Hans!"

"His son is an agent?" Tony asked.

Robbie nodded. "For the Israeli government. His name is Andrew, and he works in Jerusalem at the Holocaust memorial—Yad Vashem."

"Holey sock-a-moley!" I wheezed. (A phrase saved only for extreme circumstances.)

"Andrew is monitoring a man who has constant dealings with the memorial. A man who is a key connection to Claudio Muhtara. Andrew's assignment was to simply observe the man and stay as low-key as possible."

"So then," I broke in excitedly, "Hans gets this idea to have the Ten Brink family honored. But since the investigators do such a heavy-duty job to research the application, Andrew gets nervous about getting attention he doesn't want." I stopped to catch my breath.

Robbie looked at Tony. "Is she always like this?"

"Yep."

"Am I right?" I asked.

"You are."

I lay back on the pillows and stared up at the ceiling. Mystery solved.

"Hans didn't know his son was an agent. One month before he died, he filed the application on behalf of the Ten Brink family. It reached a committee rep who had initiated the processing before Andrew could stop it. The last thing Andrew needed was an intense investigation into his personal family history while keeping tabs on his Muhtara connection. It is unlikely his cover would have been blown, but to an under-cover agent any undue attention risks exposure. After his father died, he kept a close eye on the initial investigation in hopes they couldn't find the right Johann Ten Brink, in hopes the carving was somehow lost during the intervening fifty years. When he learned the Israeli Embassy had found a man in the United States with an old wooden carving, he sent a desperate message through highly classified communication channels: 'destroy carving.'"

Those two words dissolved the mystery-solved smile on my face. "Destroy carving." I couldn't think of a more heartless combination of words.

"Why did Kahlil want the carving then?" Tony asked.

Robbie grinned sheepishly. "That was my fault. He caught me by surprise and walked in on me when I was looking at it. I had to think fast, so I said I got a message earlier when he wasn't around that Muhtara wanted the carving. Kahlil worshiped Muhtara, so the carving became sort of an icon to him."

I hardly heard him. "Destroy carving" was still reverberating in my brain.

"Where is it, Casey?" Robbie asked quietly, not looking me in the eye.

I swallowed hard as the room got blurry. "It's not just a carving," I whispered hoarsely. "It's a shepherd boy. It means everything to Mr. Ten Brink. He doesn't care about the Avenue of the Righteous. He only wants the carving."

"I have my orders, Casey," Robbie replied gently.

"But—but you can just explain it all to Mr. Ten Brink! He'll understand! He'll keep your big secret!" I shouted back, as much to fight against the miserable ache in my throat as to protect the carving for Mr. Ten Brink. "You don't need it!"

"Yes, he does," Tony murmured.

I turned on Tony. "What are you saying?"

"Come on, Casey, listen . . . Until the carving is destroyed, Andrew is going to be afraid of being found out and blowing the whole undercover operation. His *dad* made the carving, Casey. Do you think he'd order the destruction of something like that if he didn't think it was necessary? It's for a greater good. Andrew is a good guy who's working to take down that Muhtara creep."

I knew I was defeated. But my anguished underdog mentality tried one more time. "That carving represents Hans. Don't you get it, Robbie?"

"I hate this job," Robbie muttered.

I tried hard not to think about stuffy old Mr. Ten Brink, but his face stayed in front of me even when I squeezed my eyes shut. Thick white hair brushed back and to the side. Dark glasses a generation or two out of style. A formidable bearing, marked by the cold suspicion with which he regarded everyone. Frosty blue eyes that melted like ice cubes in the sun when speaking about Holland and flowers and heroes.

It wasn't fair.

I pulled a pillow over my face. Let them think I was crying. I was. And I didn't care. I just wanted to cry privately.

I heard shuffling, and I knew Robbie was leaving. He paused before closing the door behind him.

"I really hate this job."

Chapter
Sixteen

■

I PRETENDED TO BE ASLEEP WHEN MOM, DAD, MARTY, AND JACKIE all visited later that evening. Only Tony knew I wasn't. He ushered them to the cafeteria, and I was grateful for it.

I stared at the blank gray of the TV screen in an upper corner, wondering when Robbie would be back for the carving, wondering where Alex stashed it, wondering why on earth I liked to read the classified ads. Why couldn't I have picked the sports section, like Tony? Or the comics? Now there was a worthy avenue to explore. I could transfer my addiction for the obits, lost and founds, and personals to Snoopy, Calvin and Hobbes, and Garfield.

A tap sounded at the door, and I expected Robbie to come in with a group of other local feds, demanding that I hand over the carving. I quickly shut my eyes.

"Casey? Are you sleeping?"

"No. Hi, Alex."

"Hi."

He came around the bed and lowered himself into the recliner. We didn't say anything for a long time. Just sat together in mutual misery. I liked a guy who could sit still and be quiet, be reflective. Marty jabbered a mile a minute and always had to mess with things. If it were Marty sitting there, he'd be playing with the TV remote or pushing the nurse button or telling me to order an extra-large pop with cookies and crackers. The thought made me smile.

"Tell me about Robbie," I presently said.

Alex snorted, then made a move to fold his arms in disgust, but he forgot one arm was in a cast. So he wrapped his good arm around the bad.

"Yeah, I could tell you stories about Robbie." But he didn't say anything for a while.

When he did talk, he spoke quietly. "Robbie got me off the streets. I was eleven years old, running away from a kid I stole a CD from, and I slammed right into Robbie. He grabbed me and asked me what I was running from. I tried to get away when the kid came running up, said I stole his CD. 'Did you?' Robbie asked. I nodded, scared to death 'cause he looked like—well, you know what he looks like. He made me give it back. Then he sat me on the curb and told me he needed a kid to help him run a candy store. You know . . . kids and candy. Of course I agreed.

"I was thinking he probably wanted me to run drugs for him. No big deal to me—I'd done it lots of times. But it really was a candy store. And he really wanted me to work there.

"I don't know how it happened, but we got to be friends. Real friends. He did stuff for me and my family, but he didn't act like it was a big deal. It was to me, though. I told him stuff, and he listened. The older I got, the more I saw what he tried to hide from me. The way he treated other people—sometimes not very nice. Always in front of Kahlil, so I just figured he was two-faced. Just trying to stay on Kahlil's good side."

"But you know different now," I said, defending the man who wanted to take the carving away. "You know why he acted like he did."

Alex shook his head. "You don't get it. I mean, stuff like this carving thing. If he's gonna be one way, then he should be one way. Tony told me Robbie's a *Christian*," he sneered in a way that made my heart sink. "Some Christian. Stealing stuff from old men. Lying and saying rotten things about you right in front of other people. He even killed Kahlil. Add that to his list of sins."

I considered Alex a True Blue, so I really wanted him to understand something. But first let me explain True Blue.

A True Blue is someone who . . . uh . . . let me put it this way . . . If a person doesn't laugh or clap when a student has broken a dish in the cafeteria, he's a True Blue. If a person sticks up for someone like Esther Zimmerman, she's a True Blue. If a person doesn't notice the zit on your chin or the way you stutter or who your parents are or aren't, mark that person as a True Blue.

You can tell True Blues by instinct, and I'm learning that *how* they look doesn't have much to do with it. I knew right after I told him about Hans, Gerrit, and Johann that Alex was a genuine True Blue.

So I desperately wanted him to understand what I'd only in the last hour figured out.

"I know what you mean about the Christian thing," I replied in a tone that put me on Alex's side. "To think someone could have a job like that and still be a Christian . . . yeah, right."

"Exactly."

"That's what I *thought* anyway . . . until I thought about it some more."

He looked at me with narrow, suspicious eyes. I had to pick my words extremely carefully. I didn't want him to think I'd bailed out on him.

"I mean, look at Gerrit Ten Brink. Now *there's* someone you could've counted on to be a *real man*."

Alex looked at me in surprise. "Yeah. That's kind of what I thought. Gerrit was cool."

"No doubt. He was cool, all right. Saved not only Hans, but Hans's kids. A whole generation. And he probably didn't even think about it like that."

"Maybe he did," Alex pointed out.

"True. Maybe he did. But Gerrit also lied."

"What! He didn't *lie*. In what way?"

"He lied to the Nazis. The way he faked ID papers for Hans— he even renamed the kid. The papers said the kid wasn't Jewish—just Dutch."

"Oh, come on! They were Nazis!"

"Gerrit lied even more. He and his family helped three more Jews after Hans. He lied every time he cashed in the extra ration cards he stole. And that made him a thief as well. Remind you of anyone?" Then I lowered the boom. "It's like he was undercover—just like Robbie."

Alex was on his feet, glaring like he wanted to take a swing at me. He started to pace back and forth in the room, messing up his hair with his good hand.

He stopped. "So that's what you're trying to say."

I nodded. "I don't see much difference between Gerrit Ten Brink and Robbie Burns. They weren't perfect, but God used them anyway."

Alex stood very still, then walked back over to the recliner and sat down.

I gave him time. It was a lot to swallow. Took me half a package of Oreos and a whole hour to figure that one out. And it was still a totally new concept to me. That maybe God some-times uses black leather jackets and people who aren't . . .

normal. People who are flawed and imperfect. Pastor Mullins once said God has His people, a "remnant" he called them, everywhere. For the Alex Wendells and the Phil DeWinters and the Hans VanderWeides who need them.

And it's looking to me like He isn't choosy who gets the job done, as long as the job gets done. Shoot, look at Rahab, the harlot in the Bible. Not exactly of pristine character. Or even King David. But they had a job to do, and they did it. I figure God uses those who are willing, not necessarily those who are perfect. Which, if you ask me, is a big relief.

I didn't want to say what I knew I had to say, but Duty loomed tall and relentless. I would have preferred to be reading a Starr Cassidy novel in the pool house. Or tramping through the woods with Marty, looking for bug specimens for science projects. Anything but this.

"Where's the carving, Alex?" My heart was breaking.

He looked at me sullenly and didn't answer.

"Robbie needs it, Alex. To prevent a guy at Yad Vashem from blowing his cover—Hans's son, Andrew." I think I actually heard my heart splinter.

"Yeah, yeah. Tony told me."

"Where is it?" I hate your job too, Robbie.

"But Mr. Ten Brink won't get his tree."

"I know." I know, I know!

"He deserves the tree. All the Ten Brinks do."

"I know." Oh, Alex . . .

"It ain't fair."

"It ain't."

Alex untied the top strings of his gown and reached inside. To my surprise, he pulled out a small leather bundle.

"Fits kind of nicely between me and my cast," he explained with a slight smile. He held it a moment, then handed it to me.

I stared down at the bundle, scarcely believing it lay in my hands. Respectfully, I unwrapped it.

It was small, maybe only eight inches high if I stood it on my tray. Because Mr. Ten Brink described it so well, I felt like I was seeing it for the second time. Crudely carved, yes; but even I could see the talent evident in the sculpting of the face and in the detail on the pouch slung over the shepherd's shoulder. He had a slight smile on his wooden lips, his chin tilted up and his eyes to the sky. His hands held the feet of a lamb across his shoulders, and the lamb seemed content to be there.

I imagined a pile of wood shavings at my feet and the weight of a small knife in my hand. The glide of the knife down the length of the shepherd's long garment; precise cuts to form the fingers; careful scrapes to shape the nose.

I wondered at this little wooden statue, this thing that meant very different things to very different people.

"It's beautiful," a quiet voice said at my side.

I didn't turn to acknowledge Robbie yet. I wanted to hold the carving a little while longer. For Mr. Ten Brink's sake.

"I have it here, Mr. Ten Brink. It's in my hands. You would have wanted me to see it, I know. You would have shown it to me if you could. Well, it's beautiful. I know how much it means to you, and I'll say good-bye for you."

I traced my finger down the strap of the pouch. I memorized the detail in the folds of the garment. I touched the lamb and ran my pinkie over a cheek. I turned it around in my hands, then held it upside-down to look at the bottom and found a surprise.

Carved in small, worn letters was an inscription:

VOOR JOHANN MYN VRIEND
VAN KEES

"'To Johann my friend. From Kees,'" Robbie said.

I blinked at him. "You know Dutch?"

"I know a few languages," he answered with a little smile.

He still had the look of someone without command of the English language, let alone a few others.

He didn't ask for it right away but just let me take my time, and I was grateful. I felt a little awkward with him standing right there, but I didn't want to give it up yet.

"I have one favor to ask," I said.

"Name it," Robbie replied.

"I want the rest of the Classifieds to see this before you take it away."

"No problem. I saw them in the cafeteria. I'll stop by before I leave."

"Thanks," I murmured.

I held it a minute longer to let my hands memorize the roughness and the weight of it. I offered it to Alex. He held it a long moment, then reached for the scrap of old leather and carefully wrapped it up. He gave it back to me, and I gave it to Robbie Burns.

He didn't leave right away. He looked at the two of us, and I looked back at him. I wanted to memorize him too, so I wouldn't forget.

Black sideburns, black hair slicked back into a ponytail, perfect teeth, a diamond-circled ruby in one ear, gold necklaces. The sunglasses were shoved up on his head, and it looked cool. He wore totally cool clothes, and his brown eyes held a good-guy spark in his eyes . . . eyes that could never belong to a creep.

I glanced at the hands holding the carving. Knuckles hairy as ever. I smiled then, and he smiled back.

Then he looked at Alex and said, "I'm on my way to

Washington. I'll be in town next week to get my stuff. Okay if I look you up? See, I consider you to be family, Alex. More family than I've ever had."

After a long, awkward moment Alex nodded, though he didn't look at him. I turned back to Robbie.

"I guess I never said thanks for saving my life from Kahlil."

Robbie shrugged, then grinned. "All in a day's work. Sometimes this job ain't so bad. I got to meet you two."

I looked at the small bundle in Robbie's hands. "What's going to happen to it?" I whispered.

Robbie's grin disappeared. He looked down at the bundle. "I have my orders."

"'Destroy carving,'" I said bitterly. Then I felt bad. This probably wasn't easy for Robbie. What a crummy thing to have to do.

I looked at him and wanted to say something nice, some neat parting words to stick in his head to remember me by. I tried, but I'm not easy with sentiment.

"See ya later, buzzard breath."

He laughed. Then after a long look at both of us, he gave a salute and turned to leave. He had his hand on the door.

"He doesn't care about the tree," Alex blurted out desperately. Robbie stopped but didn't turn around.

We waited breathlessly for some miracle. It wasn't supposed to end this way. He was supposed to turn around and say, "Oh man, what was I thinking! Here you go—give the carving back to Mr. Ten Brink with my regards." But he didn't.

"I have my orders," he muttered very quietly. "I—I'm sorry. I—I—" He broke off and jerked open the door. I could hear his steps in the hospital corridor. They finally faded away.

Was this the end of the story? No recovered carving for an old man? No tree on the Avenue of the Righteous? I felt like— like tearing things apart.

Alex poked at the papers sitting on my tray. "What's that stuff?" he asked in a monotone. He only said it for something to say. Maybe to prevent himself from crying. Maybe to prevent *me* from crying. "You gonna write a book about this?"

I brightened a little as I looked at my papers. At least *something* good might come out of this after all.

"No. This is the charter for our new agency. The Classifieds."

"Doesn't look like much is written down."

I grinned at him. "That's because *you* helped write it. Want me to read it to you?"

"Sure."

I picked up the first paper and cleared my throat.

"'The Classifieds. Hereby Established on the Above Aforementioned Date in the Year of our Lord. Founding members are: Casey Louise DeWinter, Anthony Edward DeWinter, Jacquelyn Rose D'Amico, and Martin Avery Behrens.'"

I picked up the next and last sheet.

"'The Classifieds are hereby established as a Secret Helper Agency. In mutually agreed upon situations, our motto is this: Help. No matter who. No matter what.' So what do you think?"

"Cool," he nodded approvingly. "Only I think you need to add something to the first sheet."

I snatched the sheet and peered at it, a little miffed. English is my best subject, and doggone it I thought it sounded pretty impressive. "Aforementioned." Not too often a person gets to write a fourteen-letter word. And yes, there *are* fourteen letters in it because I know some (as I would) will check to make sure. I counted twice.

"What's missing?" I replied in a not very curious tone.

"My middle name is Michael. And Wendell is spelled with two l's."

Chapter
Seventeen

■

I GOT OUT OF THE HOSPITAL THAT EVENING BECAUSE THEY ONLY wanted to keep me for "observation," which is weird because I didn't feel very observed. The word *observation* brings to my mind a group of med students with clipboards and thoughtful looks on their faces, jotting down notes and asking questions.

My ribs healed nicely. Getting back to my old self physically was great, though I missed the hoopla at school when the bruises on my face faded to green to yellow to normal. It was fun turning to look at someone and have them gasp and ask what happened to the other guy or if I'd just had a date with Genghis Khan.

We're a bona fide group now, the Classifieds. We have meetings and everything. Not that we have a new Situation to work on, because we're still in a tailspin from our first. So mostly we just get together and rehash old times and play board games or cards or watch a video.

I'm the president of the Classifieds. Alex is vice president (he says he doesn't want much to do), Tony is treasurer, Jackie is secretary, and Marty is secretary of war and speaker of the house (his own choices of office).

We try to meet once a week, in the pool house. Alex takes

the bus over from Selby. He even knows Gus now. And he didn't buy "Gus" as the bus driver's name either.

I think Alex is a little awed when he comes over to my house, because he's not used to things being halfway normal. He's surprised by stuff like a pot roast in the oven or a dad who isn't drunk. He once commented on how *clean* everything was, which made me throw a triumphant look at my mother because not two minutes before he came in, she'd complained about how messy the place was.

I know what you're thinking. If I were Starr Cassidy, there would be no loose ends. Mr. Ten Brink would have gotten his carving back. If I were Starr Cassidy, somehow, miraculously, a tree would be planted at Yad Vashem without any repercussions whatsoever to the life of a secret agent on the premises.

But even as Robbie Burns walked away with the carving, a tiny little hope in me refused to be squashed. Call me a diehard, but I can't believe Robbie will have the carving destroyed. Yeah, yeah, he had his orders. That's what he told us. But every once in a while for a cause noble and great, an order is ignored. Like how Gerrit Ten Brink ignored Hitler's orders. Probably this very minute in the world somewhere, an order is quietly being shunned to make way for a grand and heroic Reason. Robbie couldn't destroy the carving. Might as well torch the *Mona Lisa*.

Nope, somewhere out there the carving is safe and sound, kept unharmed until Claudio Muhtara is nabbed by the good guys and Andrew VanderWeide is no longer at risk of exposure. As I lay on my stomach on the porch watching Mr. Sanchez trim his hedges, I propped my chin on my fist and let a Dream State take care of the carving.

■ ■ ■

Someday in the hopefully not too distant future.

Mr. Ten Brink is in his living room, his hair now so white that it has a bluish tinge. He's leaning against the fireplace mantel, looking at the spot where the shepherd used to be. His wife is in a rocking chair knitting booties for their great-granddaughter.

"Give it up, Johann my dear," his wife says. "You know the carving is long gone."

Mr. Ten Brink sighs. "Yes, Gracie. And I'll never know why."

A knock sounds at the door.

Mr. Ten Brink opens it, and lo and behold, it's none other than Casey DeWinter, the girl who used to pester him for stories about the carving.

"Why, hello, Casey. My, you're looking lovely. The years have been good to you. Your hair is no longer painfully average, and I see your teeth haven't changed. You always did have splendid teeth."

"Why, thank you, Mr. Ten Brink," I say gracefully. "I stopped by to bring you something . . . It was airmailed to me with a postmark from Bora Bora. I think you'll be happy to see this." I hand him a bundle in cracked brown leather.

He opens it with trembling hands. And there, at long and impossible last, is his infinitely valuable shepherd boy.

Gasp, sputter. "My shepherd boy! Gracie, it's come home again!"

While Mr. Ten Brink and his wife celebrate to bring the roof down, I slip away, the humble heroine.

■ ■ ■

A suspicious glare from Mr. Sanchez pulled me back from the future. I blinked and glanced at the Starr Cassidy book next to me. Good old Starr would've had the carving back before the time it takes Tony to devour a baking sheet full of chocolate-chip cookies. Everything is fair in her world!

But I'll let you in on a secret. Starr Cassidy ain't normal.

Don't get me wrong. I have all thirty-seven novels and am anxiously waiting for number 38. Word has it Starr will put an end to famine in a country called Bucharania. She's my hero, she really is! She's never had a zit, and she can weave beautiful Indian baskets. One sold in an international auction for a thousand bucks. Get this—she donated the money to an Indian reservation.

Great reading. But since I live in the real world, this adventure doesn't wrap up in a pretty pink bow. Well, not quite. Burlap is more like it.

See, I got this idea.

▪ ▪ ▪

It had to be a carob tree, but to my shrieking chagrin I discovered it couldn't be. I'll explain.

I called four different greenhouses, and none of them had even *heard* of a carob tree. Then my dad suggested that I drop in on a friend of his who owns a nursery just outside Hamilton and who also happens to be the former head botanist at the Churchill Arboretum in England. This boy knew his trees.

Professor Beresford is an older man with a neatly trimmed gray beard and a vague air about him. Vague because he always focuses on a spot about three inches away from your eyes when answering questions.

"A carob tree? Dear me, no. Native to the East

Mediterranean. Cultivated elsewhere, but only in the Tropics. Could never survive a Michigan winter."

It never once occurred to me that I *couldn't* get a carob tree. Starr Cassidy would have marched into a greenhouse in Alaska and walked out with a dozen of them. And they would have survived the winters nicely.

He'd probably never had a customer so devastated about a lack of a particular tree. Professor Beresford seemed concerned.

"I say . . . would a tree in the same family do?"

"Pardon?" I answered politely despite my shatteredness.

"Why, the carob tree is a member of the *leguminosae* family."

He'd lost me, but this was sounding kind of hopeful.

"Meaning . . ." I said encouragingly.

"Meaning several species of the *leguminosae* can survive a rigorous habitat," he soundly declared with a brilliant smile and a thump of his cane on the ground.

"No kidding?" This was the best news I'd heard all year. I beamed back at him and replied with all the hope a human being can project in one sentence, "And do you happen to have one of the aforementioned species available?"

"I do!" He capered off and disappeared down a row of greenery. When he returned, he carried a sapling held by the narrow trunk near the bottom. The roots were gathered up in a burlap sack.

He placed it in front of me with a flourish.

"This, my dear, is the black locust tree, also known as the *Robinia Pseudo-Acacia*. It shall grow thirty to sixty feet high, and in May or June it sports the loveliest and most fragrant flowers this side of the Appalachians, which incidentally is where they are native, though they are cultivated in places like Michigan for ornamental purposes."

"What color are the flowers?" I asked hopefully.

"White . . . ?" he replied in a tone like a question.

I sighed. "Absolutely perfect. How much do I owe you?"

"Why, as luck would have it, we are running a special on the *Robinia Pseudo-Acacia*," he replied gallantly. "It is free with any carnation purchase."

"Sold."

Let Starr have her twelve carob trees, I sniffed as I left Beresford Nursery with a ten-pound sapling in one hand and a single white miniature carnation in the other.

I had my *Robinia Pseudo-Acacia.*

■ ■ ■

Besides me, it had to be Alex. Him alone. The other Classifieds would understand.

We stood in front of Mr. Ten Brink's home at 244 Chesterton Road at 11:42 P.M. on a Saturday night. Alex carried the shovel and a flashlight. I carried the tree.

Alex dug the hole square in the middle of Mr. Ten Brink's front lawn. We removed the burlap sack and placed the tree in the hole, then shoveled in dirt around it and tamped it down good. We stood back and surveyed our work.

"I feel like we need to say some words," Alex whispered to me, "like they would have done at the Avenue of the Righteous."

"Absolutely," I whispered back. "Ceremony is crucial."

We stood and thought a while, then Alex cleared his throat.

"For Gerrit Ten Brink and all who helped. May this tree, uh, grow forever and ever like the generations he saved. And may it be an everlasting memorial to abide . . . uh . . . ever-lastingly."

How could I compete with such poetry? So I, the wordy one, merely said, "For Johann and Hans."

I took out the special envelope I had worked on earlier in the day and taped it good to the trunk of the sapling. In it was a note I had rewritten four times—twice because I wanted to get the words right and two other times to get it as neat as possible. The paper in the envelope simply said:

> *Voor Johann Myn Vriend*
> *Van Hans*
> *and the Classifieds.*

Epilogue

■

*T*he thump on the porch announced the arrival of the *Hamilton Daily*.

Tony and I had our usual race, and I let him win because I was in a generous mood. He extracted the sports section and tossed me the classifieds. Yeah, I know. I said I'd transfer my addiction to the comics. I changed my mind. Sue me.

I flipped through the ads, noting most of them were carryovers, until my eye caught the last one. A common ad, the type I've seen frequently; but this time such an ad sparked a Dream State.

TWO TICKETS TO HOLY LAND. WALK WHERE JESUS WALKED FOR ONLY TWENTY-NINE NINETY-FIVE. CALL CHUCK AT 555-2612 AFTER 6 P.M.

I plan on going to Israel someday. My first stop will be Yad Vashem on the Mount of Remembrance, a hill just west of Jerusalem.

I'll walk among the carob trees in the Avenue of the Righteous and think about the tree planted in an old man's front yard half a world away. And it won't matter to me, really, that the tree is in Hamilton instead of Jerusalem because it didn't matter to him. He wanted the carving, not the carob tree. I found out heroes are like that.